DEAD DRAW

A PERFECT PLAY NOVEL

LAYLA REYNE

Cover Design: Cate Ashwood Designs

Cover Photography: Wander Aguiar Photography

Developmental Editing: Edits by Kristi

Line & Copy Editing: Susie Selva

Proofreading: Lori Parks

First Edition

June, 2022

E-Book ISBN: 978-1-7373524-5-7

Paperback ISBN: 978-1-7373524-6-4

Content Warnings: explicit sex; explicit language; violence; trafficking; off-page death of a former spouse; instances and/or discussion of homophobia; and instances and/or discussion of depression and PTSD.

ABOUT THIS BOOK

When a marriage of convenience is the only play left...

Special Agent Emmitt Marshall knows how to:
Wear a cowboy hat.
Hack anything.
Win at chess.
Fall in love with emotionally unavailable men.
He even knows the perfect play to catch the terrorists who
killed his mentor.

Special Agent Levi Bishop doesn't know how to:
Move on after his wife's death.
Help his grieving son.
Pay off his mountain of debt.
Fix the mess some cowboy cyber agent made of his case.
The same cowboy who proposes a marriage of convenience
to stop a common enemy.

Marsh is either the answer to Levi's prayers—or a handsome nightmare in a Stetson.

Levi doesn't know.

But both men do know their cases and lives are at a dead draw.

There's only one play left…

I do.

Dead Draw is book one of the Perfect Play m/m romantic suspense series, featuring a cocky hacker with a heart of gold, a widowed father who needs so much help, and a plan only a cowboy could cook up. Grab your hat, hold tight to the reins, and enjoy the ride!

For Kristi
Thank fuck you always know the right place to start

ONE

MARSH WAS FUCKED. He couldn't pinpoint any single moment or event when it had all gone to shit. It was more like a cascade—or an avalanche.

He grimaced at the thought. He fucking hated snow. He'd been born and raised in the Texas desert, then had spent half his life in a different desert on the other side of the world. He didn't do snow. Four years in Europe was enough. He never wanted to see the white flaky shit again if he could help it.

It had been snowing that night in Vienna. Three years ago. When the windows had rattled with the force of an explosion five kilometers away.

That moment, he could say with certainty, was when the fuckening had begun.

Had led him to this moment. A hotel room in San Diego, his computer monitors arranged on the desk so there was a sliver of Pacific Ocean visible between them. Moonlight reflected on the dark rippling water outside, same as it did across the rail yard crawling with federal agents on one of his monitors.

Across the face of the beautiful, irate federal agent whose raid Marsh had just fucked to high heaven.

"Any sign of them?" Special Agent Levi Bishop called to the other agents on-site.

With each reply of "Clear," his anger and frustration grew. Hands on his trim hips, high cheekbones swept with silvery light and rosy anger, his perfectly straight nose casting a shadow that darkened one blue eye while the other shone, Agent Bishop could be mistaken for one of those pissed-off wolf shifters in the paranormal romance books Marsh used to borrow from Camp Casey's mishmash collection of donated paperbacks.

Marsh could be forgiven a fantasy or two about subduing the wolf. Fantasies that were cut short by gunfire that ripped through the speakers and the rail yard on-screen.

Marsh lurched forward in his chair, eyes following the action. Bishop crouched, ran, and hit the ground, facedown in a nearby ditch, elbows braced, pistol aimed forward. Another agent in an FBI windbreaker, his dark hair glossy, his features sharp and focused crawled into the ditch beside him, similarly at the ready.

"Backup advance," Bishop said over the FBI comms channel Marsh also had access to. Sort of legitimately. He had *Special Agent* in front of his name too. That counted.

Gravel crunched as other agents on Bishop's periphery advanced. As if in answer, movement at the opposite end of the yard caught Marsh's attention. Caught the attention of Bishop too. "FBI! Stop right there!"

Just one step closer, Marsh silently urged.

The lone stranger stepped forward, and having hacked control of the yard's security system, Marsh flicked on the floodlight at the far end, illuminating the figure without blinding the agents.

Several agents turned, but Agent Bishop remained focused. "FBI! I said stop! Hands up!"

The man, dressed all in black, lifted his arms, a pistol in one hand, hanging upside down, his finger through the trigger guard. "Did you turn those lights on?"

"Who are you?"

"Hired security," the man said. He spread his arms wider, and that's when Marsh saw the patch on his outer right shoulder—and Bishop must have seen a similar one on his front. "Name's Anton Dale." He was an average-sized white man, midthirties maybe. Given his steady stance and surrendered weapon, Marsh guessed ex-law enforcement—in this town, probably ex-military. "What's going on?"

"Did you discharge your weapon?" Bishop asked.

"Yeah," Dale replied. "Aimed high enough not to hit anything. We've had a problem with looters lately. That why you're here?"

"Put the gun on the ground," the agent beside Bishop ordered.

Dale immediately obeyed, slow and steady. "Did you turn on the lights?" he asked again as he straightened.

"Not us," radioed the FBI agent running comms.

Bishop kept his pistol trained on Dale. "You working with someone, Mr. Dale?"

"No, just me." He raised his hands a little higher, spread his fingers a little wider, the first signs of distress. "Just clocked in. What's going on? Who turned on the lights?"

"Any other movement?" Bishop asked.

"All clear," came word over the comms.

Judging Dale wasn't a threat, Agent Bishop stood. "Security was supposed to be off tonight. We're running an operation."

"No one told me."

"Someone clearly told our suspects," said a familiar voice over the comms. "And I have an idea on the lights." Marsh grimaced again. She was going to be extra pissed when she confirmed it was him. Would bust his balls like she used to in the desert. "Agent Bishop, finish sweeping the area," she said. "Determine if your traffickers were ever there, then report back to command. We'll track down the cyber breach on our end."

She signed off and so did Marsh. He'd heard enough. His gambit hadn't worked. Instead of forcing Agent Bishop's traffickers, who were tied to Marsh's terrorists, into action, he'd spooked them from acting at all. Or they'd diverted a direction neither he nor Agent Bishop's team had covered.

He closed his laptops, picked up his phone, and stepped out onto the balcony. He could call his best friend on the East Coast and, despite it being the middle of the night, make Sean listen to him verbally facepalm. Or he could call his other best friend on the West Coast at a slightly more decent hour, likewise bemoan his idiocy, then activate the hackers at Brax's disposal, including the one who, at this hour, was either in bed beside him or on his own computers running an op for his family's organization.

And Brax knew better than anyone the shit he'd just stepped into. Marsh opened his favorites list and tapped on the grizzled mug he used to have a crush on.

Brax answered on the second ring. "It's one in the morning," he mumbled groggily.

Marsh didn't mince words. "I went cowboy and fucked up a raid for one of Eagle's agents."

"Well, you're fucked."

"Tell me something I don't already know." Marsh wrapped his fingers around the balcony rail and leaned against the sturdy iron, letting it hold his tired, heavy weight. "Now, get your husband on the line and help me sort a way to unfuck this mess. Please."

♙♙♝♟♟♟♟♞♙♙

"*YOUR TRAFFICKERS WERE TIPPED OFF.*"

Hours later, Levi's ASAC's words still rang in his ears. He pulled into his garage, turned off the car, and lowered the door on the rising sun.

Eighteen months of grueling work ruined.

They'd cleared the rail yard, cleared Mr. Dale, and once back at the office, cleared the security interference. Levi couldn't ever recall seeing his ASAC so angry. Some cyber jockey—or as the ASAC kept calling him "that fucking cowboy"—on the Bureau's legal attaché team at The Hague had tipped off the traffickers. Special Agent Marshall had been trying to help supposedly. He'd also been the one to tip off Levi's ASAC about the rail yard, thinking some cyber bullshit he'd pulled would force Levi's traffickers' hand. Agent Marshall wanted to get at someone higher up the ladder, his ASAC had said. Well, all Agent Marshall had done was aid and abet the kidnapping of ten women.

Help.

Levi's bitter laugh was almost as sharp as the horn that blew when he punched the steering wheel. He'd had a plan to intercept the traffickers at one of three known handoff spots next week. They'd moved the location and timing of the op based on Agent Marshall's tip. And now the traffickers would surely change their game plan, picking a new transfer location that wasn't potentially being surveilled.

Eighteen months of long days and nights gone up in smoke.

More victims snatched out of their lives and gone missing.

His wife's legacy—

David opened the door at the far end of the garage, his flannel bottoms and Lakers tee wrinkled, his green eyes narrowed, and his ginger hair sticking out in every direction. "Was that necessary?" he grumbled in surly fourteen-year-old.

Levi grabbed his phone off the dash and climbed out of the SUV, soreness setting in from the quick drop onto hard ground at the rail yard. He worked out regularly, ran several miles a day, but thirty-eight was thirty-eight. "Sorry about that."

"Are you just getting home?"

Levi checked the time on his phone. "Go back to bed. You've got another hour before your alarm goes off."

"I'm turning it off." David flapped a dismissive hand his direction. "Just for that."

"Your aunt will be here at eight to pick you up for work."

More grumbling as he turned back in the direction of his cave, the door slamming shut, the Keep Out sign rattling on its nail.

The alarm reminder was selfish on Levi's part. They'd maybe get an hour together before Nicole picked him up. It would be the most time they'd spent together all week, the raid prep nonstop ever since Agent Marshall's useless tip had unnecessarily advanced their timeline. Levi missed his son.

He unlocked the other door and entered the house, Taco greeting him enthusiastically as soon as he opened the pet gate and turned the corner for the kitchen. "Shush, boy. David's already grumpy." The rescued racing greyhound muffled his barks, offering pitiful whines instead as he shook his tall slender body, tail whipping Levi's legs. "Yes, I know, I love you too." He ran a hand along his narrow fawn head and scratched behind his ears. "You want an early breakfast?"

The whining escalated, bordering on a bark again, which Levi shushed with a boop to his nose. Only to be foiled by a plaintive *meow* as Burrito slunk into the kitchen and wound around her bestie's legs, nipping at Taco's ankles until he moved to the feeding mat. A little of the night's weight lifted off Levi's shoulders at their playful interactions, at their eagerness for Levi's attention and the sustenance he could give them. Lifted a little more as he straightened from setting their bowls down and watched the birds outside the patio door, finches swarming the feeders and the usual trio of doves tottering around on the ground beneath them. Lifted more at the folded blankets, the slipcovers arranged, the dishes done—

Then plummeted at the stack of mail on the end of the kitchen island. He flipped through the envelopes, too many with *Past Due* stamped on them, and froze when he reached the last one. Past Due was stamped on it too along with

Notice of Repossession. He glanced at the return address—
the collection agency the car loan had been referred to. He'd
sold his hybrid last year to pay hospital bills. He'd kept
Kristin's SUV since it was roomier, but he'd fallen behind
on the payments. He flipped it over, saw it had been
opened, then slowly turning around, took in the kitchen
and living room area anew, seeing the order for what it was
—his son's attempt to lessen the blow, even though it had to
have been a blow to him too.

On this day of all days…

Levi tossed the envelope onto the pile, leaned back
against the island, covered his face with his hands, and
silently screamed.

It was all going to shit.

TWO

"MARRY ME."

Levi lifted his gaze from his plate of untouched food and nearly spit out his champagne. Sliding into the chair across from him was the largest, most attractive man he'd ever seen. And the most underdressed in the room. Faded jeans, a shiny belt buckle, red-checked flannel, and a snow-white Stetson had no business among the designer threads of San Diego's finest.

Neither did Levi with his maxed-out credit cards and no-name sports coat, but traditions mattered. Just because his other half was no longer on this earth didn't mean he shouldn't celebrate the years they'd lived and loved together—here, in this place where sixteen years ago they'd toasted their vows with friends and family. After the shitty few days Levi had had, he deserved to wallow with the best champagne as his company.

And this cowboy apparently.

Wait, *cowboy*… It couldn't be…

"Did I steal your words, Agent Bishop?" the handsome

stranger with the Texas accent drawled. Bronze skin spoke of a lifetime in the sun, warm brown eyes were punctuated by deep laugh lines, his dark, silver-flecked beard dusted a chiseled jaw, and teeth as white as his hat dug into his full lower lip. "The only one I need is *yes*."

Levi glanced at the bottle of champagne in the sterling silver ice bucket beside him. He'd only drunk half. Nowhere near enough to get him tipsy. Nowhere near enough to make him hallucinate the mountain of a man across from him or the fact that Mount Cowboy knew his name. Or that what he was proposing was absurd. There was only one explanation. He lowered the flute to the table, careful not to form an angry fist around the stem and shatter the delicate crystal. "Agent Marshall, I presume?"

"Brains and beauty." The cowboy withdrew a leather wallet from his back pocket and tossed it onto the table. A familiar brass badge twinkled under the restaurant's chandeliers, next to a badge that read Special Agent Emmitt Marshall.

Levi folded his arms and clutched his biceps to keep from swinging. "So you're the asshole who cratered my investigation."

Agent Marshall raised both hands, palms out. "I was trying to help."

Levi scoffed. "Get a better definition of *help*."

"That's why I'm here." He pushed up his rolled shirtsleeves and leaned forward, resting his forearms on the table. Golden-brown skin stretched over corded muscle, and Levi almost missed what Agent Marshall said next. "Our teams can't seem to coordinate, but you and I, we could make it work."

The absurdity of the notion brought Levi screeching

back to reality. "You don't have a team," he said. "And, last I heard, you don't have a case either since you can't do your job without alerting the targets."

"I needed the money to show their hand."

Levi lurched forward, palms smacking the table loud enough to make himself cringe. Loud enough to check his volume before his words came out as a yell. "And I needed to get those traffickers behind bars before they trapped more victims."

"Our goals aren't mutually exclusive if we work together."

Levi shoved to his feet and threw his napkin on the table, beyond pissed this fucking cowboy had ruined his operation and further ruined his forever-ruined evening. "You're a fucking lunatic."

"Maybe." Agent Marshall's hand wrapped around his wrist, stalling his retreat, and Levi's eyes shot to the dark ones dancing beneath the Stetson's brim. "But I'm also your type." He tightened his grip, a callused thumb pressing against the underside of Levi's wrist, stroking his thrum-ming pulse. "Hacker, remember?" His voice dropped an octave. "And there's plenty on your personal computer to prove it."

Levi's stomach plummeted at the same time his dick began to plump. He wrenched his wrist free and sank into his chair, his knees threatening to give way. Either from lust or dread, Levi wasn't sure, the two instincts threatening to strangle him and strangling his words. "You wouldn't." He was out as pansexual, but he'd rather not have the details of his sex life combed through by a stranger, or worse, leaked to the wrong person.

"I won't if you marry me."

"That seems a bit extreme."

Agent Marshall lowered his voice, not the sexy rumble from before, more a conspiratorial whisper. "I also know you're up to your eyeballs in debt, thanks to this country's asinine healthcare system and a mortgage you can't afford on your own."

And that wasn't even counting the other bills. "I'll manage."

The other agent talked over Levi's rehearsed reply. "I came into some money last year. Money I want nothing to do with. Gave some away. The rest is burning a hole in my conscience."

"I don't want your dirty money."

"My old man was an asshole but a rich one. The money's clean and more than enough to help a good father pay his debts and keep his burgeoning delinquent in the best schools."

Levi ignored the first flicker of hope he'd felt in two years and focused instead on the lingering thread of anger and the endless string of questions unfurling between them. How much did this cyber agent know? And if he was good enough to hack Levi's computer and God only knew what other databases—banks, hospitals, public schools—then why hadn't he found another way to get to the traffickers' bankroll? Was this bonkers scheme really the last resort?

"I go back to extreme," Levi said. "You're proposing what? To be my pretend husband?"

"Not pretend. Actual husband."

"The FBI—"

"Doesn't strictly forbid relationships between agents. There are disclosure requirements, but those are primarily to protect subordinates from supervisors. Shouldn't be an issue for us."

He had an answer for everything. All cooked up in less than a day? Levi retrieved the bottle of champagne and refilled his glass, dousing the persistent flicker of hope, only to curse himself when it flared brighter. "So you're proposing an actual marriage of convenience? Offering to pay off my debts if I keep you close to this case? Why, Agent Marshall?"

Humor fled, replaced by grit and determination, by a shadow of loss and sadness that streaked across Agent Marshall's handsome features. That stole Levi's breath. "Because your traffickers do business with the same fuckers who do business with the terrorists who killed my mentor and friend three years ago, and I am so fucking tired of chasing these assholes."

Oh.

Levi's broken soul recognized the one across from him.

"You get me," Marshall correctly surmised. "You're tired too."

So fucking tired. Tired of the dead ends and near misses, tired of the relentless pace and long hours, tired of being away from his son when he needed him most, tired of the past-due bills and collection agency calls. Tired of doing it all by himself. Sighing, he slumped in his chair and downed the rest of his champagne.

Victory swept across Agent Marshall's face, chasing away the weary sadness and bringing the twinkling mirth back to his eyes. "If we have to take extreme measures so we can close these cases and get on with our lives, then fuck it." One corner of his mouth hitched into a devilish smirk. "Time to cowboy up, Agent Bishop."

Levi closed his eyes and rested his face in his hand, a muffled "Jesus" sneaking out from behind his palm.

A moment later, the Stetson landed on his head, tea tree oil and leather teasing his senses, warm breath tickling his ear. "Not Jesus, just Marsh, and I'll take that as a yes."

THREE

IF LEVI'S PARENTS' Pacific Beach home had been cramped as a kid, it was beyond cramped now that he and his three sisters were grown with kids of their own. Which was why when he and Kristin had bought their home in Rancho Peñasquitos with its open living areas, chef's kitchen, expansive backyard, and canyon vistas, family nights had moved from PB to PQ.

"How much longer on the affogato?" his mother shouted from the patio table outside.

"Working on it," Levi hollered back through the open windows. He secured the porta-filter, hit Start, then as the espresso machine whirred to life, poked his head around the kitchen wall to check on the kids in the great room. "Everyone good?"

David, on the sectional in front of the TV, gestured in the air with a controller. "Yeah, Dad." He and Bella's two teens were racing for position in whatever game they were playing on the Xbox.

Alexis, Amy's high school senior, smiled at him from the

dining table where she was helping Madelyn, Nicole's daughter, color. "We're good, Uncle Levi."

"Just holler if you need anything."

The kids returned to their own worlds, and Levi took the hint, returning to the adult one where his internal dread continued to rise. His mother still hadn't brought up the reason she'd called this gathering, but once she did, Levi would be the center of unwanted attention. Maybe she'd forget about it? Unlikely, but a single son could hope. Could also put an extra shot of amaretto in his mother's mug of gelato and espresso. He finished filling mugs and loaded them onto a tray with spoons and napkins.

He hefted the tray onto his shoulder, a holdover from his serving days, and started for the back door. The phone in his pocket vibrated with an incoming text. He had a good idea from whom. Similar texts had been popping up since Friday night on an encrypted app that had mysteriously appeared on his device. Every time a text appeared, Levi was thrown into a storm of pissed off, mildly impressed, and more than a little curious, but that confusing typhoon would have to wait, his mother's "Ice cream's melting!" insistent.

Half sighing, half chuckling, he hustled outside to the patio where his parents and siblings were gathered. The June gloom had burned off earlier in the day, leaving behind a warm Sunday afternoon and giving them more room to spread out around the long oval table.

"Finally," his mother huffed.

"I don't know," Levi teased as he set the tray out of her reach. "What did you do to deserve this?"

She leveled him with eyes the same bright blue as his own. "Levi Morelli Bishop, I spent thirty hours in labor with you. That's thirty tacked on to the forty-eight I spent birthing your sisters. That's more than enough."

"Margaret," his father gently chided.

She ignored him like the kids had ignored Levi. "And that's just the beginning!"

Levi failed to keep a straight face. Laughing, he handed her the extra-loaded mug and dropped a kiss on her head. "I'm just giving you a hard time, Mom. You more than deserve it." She cursed him for being an overgrown brat and swatted his side, but her lips curved into a smile around the first spoonful of her favorite dessert. He passed out the remaining mugs and enjoyed the five minutes of peace and quiet before reality crashed the party.

"Your cousin June's wedding is in two weeks," his mother said.

If their family was big, his mother's sister's was bigger. June was the last of Aunt Liz's six children to marry. In June. On the nose, and Liz was leaning into it hard. Not surprising as it was her last chance to one up Margaret. They loved each other fiercely, but their sibling rivalry was equally intense, made worse by the fact Aunt Liz had married for money while Levi's mom had married for love. He didn't have to be an FBI agent to know which sister was happier, and he was happy to be on the more loving side of the family. His mother harped, but it came from a good place, a heart that wanted her kids to be as happy and settled as she was.

"I want everyone on their best behavior," Margaret said as she glared at Nicole and her husband across the table.

"What?" Levi's youngest sister squawked.

"Try not to let Madelyn swim in the fountain this time."

"She's a seven-year-old. How do you propose I stop her?"

"Figure it out."

His sister's gaze skipped to him, her head starting its excited bobble, her voice sweetly cajoling. "Levi, you can watch her, yeah? She can be your date."

Fuck.

Their mother's attention swung his direction. "About that."

He swallowed down the dread and feigned ignorance. "What did I do?"

"Nothin'. That's the problem."

"Mom," his oldest sister, Amy, cajoled. "Let it—"

She talked right over her. "You can't go stag."

"I won't," Levi said. "David will be my date."

"Your mother's right," his dad, the Judas, said. "It's time to get back out there. It's been two years."

"I've been out there." On several dates, none of which warranted a second, but that was beside the point.

A point none of his family wanted to acknowledge. "There's a cute new engineer on my team at the base," Bella offered. "Recently divorced. Nice gal."

"*Or,*" Nicole said with a sly smile, "there's a gorgeous new enby at the yoga studio. Just moved here from San Francisco."

"God, no," Amy groaned. "All they'll do is gripe about the hard water and the fries in our burritos."

Nicole's husband nodded. "She's right, babe."

"Too true," Nicole conceded.

Levi offered another alternative. "I can just not go."

His mother's voice cut like a knife. "Absolutely not."

His dad's softer words sliced deeper. "June would be devastated."

He was right. Levi and June were each the youngest siblings of their families and had been practically inseparable as kids, several years behind any of their respective siblings but only a year apart themselves. She was the first person he'd come out to and the first person he'd told about Kristin's cancer diagnosis. He couldn't not be there for her, especially after the string of duds she'd been through on her way to finding Prince Charming.

"Levi doesn't have to have a date to the wedding," Amy said. "He doesn't have to date at all if he doesn't want to."

"Amy—" he tried to interject.

But their mom was on a roll. "Where's Courtney when I need her to keep you in line?"

"On shift at the hospital," Amy replied. "And my wife is not your lackey."

While the two most hardheaded of their lot snapped back and forth at each other, Levi stood and began gathering cups. "I'm going to take these in and check on Taco. He's awfully quiet."

The squabbling continued behind him as he rinsed the mugs, put them in the dishwasher, then ducked out the side door to the fenced-in dog run. Taco was stretched out in the filtered sunlight of the mesquite tree with Burrito tucked against his side. Levi lowered himself next to them and scratched behind the tabby's ears. She hissed at the disturbance and curled tighter against Taco's side, burying her face under his arm.

"Nice," Levi muttered. "Now you're mad at me too."

"Mom's not mad at *you*," Amy said as she slipped through the metal gate at the end of the run. "She's mad at *me* now, so you're welcome." She kicked off her flip-flops and sat beside him, legs crossed. "As for the wedding, just bring David and call it a day."

"And spend the entire time answering *when are you getting back out there* questions and fielding people's looks of pity?" He wanted to be there for June, he really did, but this was the first big family event since Kristin's death, and he was not looking forward to it.

"Okay, then, we've got two weeks to find you a date."

"I've already got one."

Amy's head whipped around so fast the salt-and-pepper curls of her pixie cut bounced. "Say what now?"

The earlier storm still raged around Agent Marshall, but Levi couldn't deny the appeal of the cowboy-sized life raft. Granted, any decision to accept Marsh's crazy proposal should've been based on Levi's case or on the pile of bills he'd moved to his desk upstairs, but it was the thought of all those questions and pitying looks, of the worry under-lying his parents' and siblings' voices, that made him reach for the life raft and force out the words.

He lifted a hand, pinky finger extended. "You gotta keep a lid on it." Amy was the only one of his sisters he'd trust with this; she was also the one he was closest to, despite the decade between them. He needed to tell someone—as much as he could—and he needed someone to tell him this was a bonkers scheme he should run from, not toward.

She hooked her pinky around his. "Secret's safe with me."

"So there's this other agent, Marsh, whose case is sort of connected to mine, but he fucked up, and he's off his case, and now I'm his best bet for catching the bad guys we're both after, but we can't team up officially, so he's proposed marriage." He took a deep breath and kept going before he talked himself out of this. "I keep him close, and he uses his recently inherited fortune to pay off my debts."

Levi barely avoided rolling his eyes at the whole ridiculous situation, at the ridiculous position he found himself in, at the ridiculous incompetence that should've convinced him to say no but that seemed to be fighting a losing battle against his ridiculous pride and his withering soul that couldn't take another hit.

Beside him, a wide-eyed Amy had splayed her fingers over her mouth, holding in God only knew what sounds.

"I'm guessing by that reaction you think I'm crazy."

"I do, but it's fucking perfect." She lowered her hands and clasped his. "It'll make Mom happy, get everyone off your back for a bit, and get you debt free, which I reiterate, any of us would also gladly help you with."

He squeezed her hands. "Thank you, but I'm not going to ask that of any of you. Money's tight all around."

"We can make it work."

He sidestepped the argument they'd been having the past two years and cast his gaze toward the back patio, a different argument looming. "If I get married without her there..."

"Mom already had the big fancy wedding for her precious baby boy." She flicked a hand in the air. "Tell her you eloped this time, that you didn't want to overshadow June's big day. Promise her a big Christmas wedding redo or some shit like that."

"Why would I make that promise? It's not real." If he and Marsh were lucky, their cases would be closed long before Christmas, Marsh would go back to The Hague,

Levi's debts would be paid off, a divorce would be in the works, and their lives would return to normal.

Apart.

Lonely.

Amy shrugged a shoulder. "Just a thought."

"You can stop having those now."

"Is he hot?"

Inside, the house phone rang, and Levi was happy for the excuse to end the conversation. "I should go get that."

The ringing stopped, and David's muffled voice drifted out the window. Amy snagged Levi's wrist, dragging him back on topic. "David's got it. Now answer my question. Is this Marsh guy hot?"

"Would it matter?" Amy had broken up with vanity decades ago. She was usually the last person to care about appearances. Why now?

"I don't care," she confirmed. "But Aunt Liz will if you show up to the last wedding of our generation with a hot as shit new husband."

She wasn't wrong. Maybe that small victory would be enough to also win his mother's forgiveness for eloping. He stood, hauled Amy up by the wrist, and begrudgingly whispered the truth. "He's the hottest man I've ever seen."

Her snort of laughter collided with a piercing wail from inside, startling Taco awake and jostling free a rudely awoken Burrito, who in turn hissed at a frantic Alexis who came barreling out the side door.

Amy gathered her daughter to her side. "What's wrong?"

"David called Maddie a wanker and shook his controller at her."

The brief balloon of levity popped, and reality crashed

the party once more. *Fuck*. Levi scrubbed a hand over his face. "Is David still inside?"

Alexis nodded. "Maddie ran to her mom out back."

Amy's glare was almost as frightening as their mother's. "Maybe having Marsh around will do your son some good too."

Or maybe it would backfire... spectacularly.

♟♙♗♙♙♙♙♕♙♙

FAMILY NIGHT DISINTEGRATED AFTER THAT, Levi's lack of a love life no longer the hottest topic of conversation. Though maybe that topic was an easier one than his son's behavior and the resulting lack of confidence in his mother's eyes. She stood behind the open car door, her gaze flicking between him and the house where David was. "You sure you don't want me to talk to him?"

"I've got it, Mom."

"Do you?" Hand cradling his cheek, she swiped a thumb under his left eye as if she could rub away the dark circle there. "You look tired."

Tired was an understatement made more so by the ups and downs of the weekend, the last fifteen minutes of it the lowest. "It was a long week." The longest in two years, but if he confessed that feeling, his mother would never leave.

His dad saved him the lie. "M, we should let him finish cleaning up so he can get some rest." Rest probably wasn't in the cards, but Levi took the out.

He bent and glanced around his mother's side, catching his father's eye from the driver's seat. "Thanks again for letting him crash with you Friday. I didn't want him to be alone that night."

"You shouldn't have been either," his mom said as he straightened. "We want to help, Levi. You just have to let us."

He didn't trust his voice not to shake, so he nodded, kissed her cheek, and closed the car door once she was safely inside. He waved goodbye to his dad and waited for their car to clear the corner before turning back to the house. And promptly stalled, breath as shaky as his voice, unprepared for the simmering teenager inside and the lecture he needed to give.

An adjustment, Kristin reminded in his head. *Assholes give lectures. We will not be asshole parents like mine were.*

His phone vibrated again, and this time Levi leapt at the opportunity to procrastinate a few seconds more. He opened the messaging app and read the latest texts from Marsh.

Longhorn: King cake > honey cake > stollen.

Longhorn: We met last December when you were in the Bay Area for work. I was there celebrating Hanukkah with Brax.

Brax, a former army buddy, was one of Marsh's best friends. Sean, a former FBI colleague, was the other. Just two of the many biographical bits Marsh had peppered him with in dozens of texts since Friday. He was introducing himself… and also laying the groundwork for a relationship that had quickly led to marriage. A partner should know who their spouse's best friends were—and apparently, also their seasonal cake preferences.

Levi hadn't replied to any of Marsh's texts. Did he even need to? He assumed the cyber agent was at least competent enough to hack the additional details he needed. Marsh already knew about his trip to San Francisco, his trafficking case, his piles of bills, his desires that hadn't been satisfied in over two years. Not that marrying Marsh would satisfy them either. Any arrangement they agreed to would have to be strictly professional. Levi didn't have the time or energy for more; he was already running on fumes.

He flipped the phone in his hand, debating his reply. Debating whether to reply at all. Despite what he'd told Amy, the deterioration of the evening had him waffling again. Was more change what David needed? A new stepdad was probably not a good idea, but the changes David did need—Levi around more, their lives financially stable—seemed out of reach without Marsh.

From inside, dishes clanked, water gushed, and David cursed. Levi pocketed the phone and pressed pause on his internal conflict. He'd debate the future later after settling today's crisis. He scrubbed his hands over his face, resisted a scream, and headed inside, picking up in the great room on his way to the kitchen. He grabbed a dry towel and joined his son at the sink.

"Wanker?" he said after a few minutes washing and drying once he was calm and confident enough to proceed with an adjustment and not a lecture.

"You're the one who made me watch all those British comedies."

"You can't call your cousin a wanker."

"But she is."

"No, she's a seven-year-old kid, but that's beside the point. You shouldn't call *anyone* a wanker."

"Even if they are?"

"Even if they are like you were at that age." Levi

covered David's hand, halting his scrubbing and making sure he was paying attention to this next adjustment in particular. "Did you shake your controller at her?"

Levi was heartened to see regret stain his son's down-turned face. He understood what he'd done was wrong. "I didn't mean to," he said. "I was just angry."

"About what?"

"That was the collection agency on the phone." The call David had answered when Levi was outside with Amy. "They're gonna repo the RX if you can't make the payments by Friday."

Levi withdrew his shaking hand from his son's, hoping David didn't notice. He hadn't expected a follow-up call, especially on a weekend. He'd hoped to handle it, some-how, before the threatened repo. He definitely didn't want David to have to hear any more about it. "I can get a car from the Bureau pool."

David's voice was barely audible over his angry scrub-bing. "But it was Mom's."

Levi had been wrong earlier. *This* was the lowest point of the past week. How did he reassure his son it would all be okay—that they wouldn't lose the car or the roof over their heads—when one of the last things he'd promised Kristin was to never lie to David?

"You should do it," David said.

"Do what?"

"Marry that guy."

Levi bobbled a skillet. "What guy?"

"The one you were telling Aunt Amy about."

"You weren't supposed to hear that."

"I heard enough." He handed Levi the last pan and

turned off the water. "It's not betraying Mom if you don't love him."

Levi finished drying the pan, set it on the island, and angled toward his son. "Someday I might." He thought to leave it at that, then realized how his reply sounded, how falling in love with Marsh was out of the question and too soon for him or David to even entertain. "Not Marsh, but someday I might find someone I love as much as I loved your mother."

"But that's not our problem now, is it? If this Marsh guy helps us keep the house and car, then do it. They're all we have left of her."

Levi's chest ached, and it was all he could do to draw breath, to force words out around the knot in his throat. "David, that's not all we have."

Tears escaped his woeful green eyes. "I forget a little more each day."

Levi curled him into his chest and buried his face in his son's tangle of ginger hair. "I won't let you lose anything else," he vowed, knowing he'd do anything to keep that promise, including agreeing to some crazy cowboy's proposal. He had to.

FOUR

"MARSH! WHERE'S SOPHIE?"

The panic in Sean's voice sent fear racing up Marsh's spine. He spun in his office chair, then almost fell out of it at the sight of his disheveled colleague. Sean had left the embassy hours ago, his usual too-attractive, put-together self. The man in front of him now looked like he'd just rolled out of whatever bed he'd fallen into—sadly not Marsh's. Jacket and tie gone, dress shirt and pants wrinkled, wool overcoat and dark hair sprinkled with snow. But more jolting than all that was the blatant fear in his bright blue eyes. Marsh bolted out of his chair and across the room, overwhelming worry for the man who'd become one of his closest friends over the past year, who'd made his transition out of the army and into civilian life bearable. "Sean, what's wrong?"

"Where's Sophie?"

Foreboding knotted Marsh's insides. Sean had asked that question before, right when he'd appeared, but Marsh had been too distracted by Sean's rumpled appearance and his concern for the man. "On her way to the opera house." One of the international organizations in town was holding a gala to raise awareness for its initiatives to combat human trafficking. Since their legat team was in Vienna coordinating with Interpol and the Federal Police, Sophie, the head of their team, had netted an invite to the gala. "What's wrong?"

"Did she take the U-Bahn?"

Marsh nodded.

What little color was left in Sean's face fled. Marsh grabbed his forearm to hold him steady. "Sean, what's going on?"

"Tip from one of our CIs. ISIS-backed group out of the Balkans is looking to make a statement. They can't get near the opera house—"

"But Karlsplatz and the U-Bahn are right there. Fuck!" Marsh darted back to his computers, kicking aside the desk chair for Sean to sit while he worked standing, opening windows and accessing surveillance feeds as fast as his fingers could type. "We're supposed to be getting intel from the Federal Police on all transnational organized crime and terrorist activity in the area." The whole reason their Hague-based team was in Vienna, crashing another legat's territory, was to establish a TOC task force. "How did they miss this?" How had *he* missed it?

"With what money?" Frustration added a sharp edge to Sean's fear. "Congress couldn't stop bickering long enough to pass a budget. Our government's shut down. We're not paying our bills, and the cyber-training budget is gone. Info channels are closed."

"Not to me." He'd designed the cyber upgrades—surveillance, alerts, grabs, tripwires—the local authorities had recently put in place. He could tiptoe through them better than anyone. He opened door number one to live surveillance feeds of Karlsplatz Station, started facial recognition running, and moved that window to his desktop monitor. "Keep an eye out for Sophie."

Sean wheeled to his side, eyes on the live feed, while shouting into his phone. "Dammit, Sophie. Pick up!"

Marsh opened door number two on his laptop screen… to a backlog of untagged surveillance and alerts. "Fuck! Did you alert the police?" he asked Sean. "The other legat team?" Ross, the legal attaché assigned to Vienna, was also attending the gala.

"Ross isn't answering either. Wagner's on it for the Federal Police." A small blessing. The British ex-pat was former RAF and a good cop. Their teams had worked well together. Wagner trusted them, and he wasn't the sort to sit on information or ignore a threat just because the money wasn't there. He'd put himself on the front line if he had to.

Marsh scanned the time stamps on the backlog of files until he found the most recent grab. He opened the PDF—a wire transfer confirmation from three days ago. The routing and account numbers rang familiar. He fed them into his search engine, ran it against the evidence in one of his collections, and seconds later, it returned a match. "Sean, look at this." Marsh gestured at the PDF open on the left side of his laptop screen. "That's a wire transfer from three days ago." He pointed at the other document his search had produced. "That's a wire transfer we tied to a transnational organization of interest in a human trafficking investigation."

"Same bank," Sean said, confirming what Marsh had noticed.

He ran the routing number through another collection. *Bingo*! He opened a third document. "Same bank that funded that arms deal we derailed two months ago."

Sean leaned forward in the chair, peering at the screen. "The account numbers are close too." Sean's phone vibrated at the same time facial recognition pinged a match from the surveillance feeds. Sophie, phone to her ear, had just stepped off the U-Bahn at one end of the platform. "Sophie, thank fuck, we've been trying to reach you. You need to get out of there."

"What's going on?" their legat asked.

Another match pinged. A twenty-something man, white with dark hair, cleared the bottom of the stairs at the other end of the platform. A rap sheet appeared on-screen next to his image. Peter Bauer, an Austrian citizen, arrested and charged last year with possession of narcotics with known ties to ISIS. Marsh glanced again at the surveillance. Peter's trench coat was three sizes too big.

And was that a trigger in his white-knuckled fist?

Marsh barely had time to shout "Get down!" in the direction of the phone, to throw an arm over Sean's shoulders and drag him to the floor before an explosion five kilometers away shook the embassy windows.

And shook Marsh awake.

Disoriented at first, he couldn't sort why Sean wasn't beside him, why he wasn't on the floor in the borrowed office at the embassy, why he was warm instead of cold, and why the ocean was right outside his window, albeit slightly out of focus. But then the fog of memory receded, and reality returned. He was in San Diego, in a hotel room overlooking the Pacific, in June, ten thousand kilometers and three years away from that awful winter's night in Vienna. The night his friend and mentor had been killed.

He sat up in bed, bent his knees, and propped his elbows on the aching joints. Head in his hands, he raked his fingers through his hair to shake loose the cobwebs of another night's restless sleep. When that didn't work, he rolled out of bed and shuffled over to the in-room coffeemaker. He packed it full, set it to brew, then cleaned up in the bathroom while it percolated.

He snagged the bottle of ibuprofen, his phone off the charger, his glasses, and the steaming cup of joe on his way to the desk. Still no return texts from Levi. He ignored the twinge of disappointment and concerned himself with their cover instead. All weekend, he'd been filling Levi in on himself and their "relationship." The sort of things a person should know about their fiancé. But information needed to flow both directions. Was Levi silent because he wasn't on board with the plan? He'd seemed to be coming around at the end of their conversation at the restaurant, but that was three days ago. Had he changed his mind? If Levi was still game, Marsh needed to know more about him than what a background check and basic hack had turned up.

Levi Morelli Bishop, born and raised in San Diego. Criminal justice major at San Diego State, joined the San Diego Police Department after graduation, was recruited by the FBI a few years later. Excelled at the Academy, was assigned to the San Diego field office, amassed numerous commendations, and was appointed head of the field office's human trafficking task force.

And preferred to bottom, per the porn links uncovered in his browser history.

A real Boy Scout, though he didn't have Sean's clean-cut

Boy Scout appearance. Nor was he a prickly pine like Brax, spindly and grizzled. No, Levi Bishop was pin-up worthy. Teenage Marsh would've ripped his picture out of a magazine and hidden it in his sock drawer. Levi was well proportioned for his just shy of six-foot frame, not overly bulky, a compact wall of sculpted muscle worthy of a billboard with dark blond hair, piercing blue eyes, cheekbones for days, and inviting bowed lips. But the fact Levi could be an underwear model had nothing to do with why Marsh had watched him for over an hour at that restaurant Friday night. The heartbroken sadness that surrounded Levi painted the already beautiful picture a stunning, lonesome shade.

A color Marsh knew well.

Between his palpable grief, his family, and his work, Levi was the definition of emotionally unavailable. That should've been enough to convince Marsh to keep his distance. Except emotionally unavailable men were his weakness. Maybe knowing upfront this time would make a difference. He could be Levi's husband and not fall for him. He'd learned his lesson with Brax and Sean. He'd figured out too late that he didn't stand a chance, that their hearts would always belong to other people—to two other people in Sean's case. Levi's heart was still tangled up with Kristin's. Pretending to be his husband couldn't be more. Their cover could be only that, a means for solving their cases and getting justice for Sophie. Marsh couldn't let it be more.

Assuming Levi was on board.

Marsh set aside his mug and opened the text thread to Levi, considering something that might startle the other agent into a response. **My favorite color is magenta**.

Wolfy: I did not expect that.

Bingo! **My mom loves bougainvillea. It's all over our ranch in Texas.**

A slight delay, then, **Mine's green.**

Longhorn: I know. Your old car, the front door of your house, the color theme on your computer. Your son's and late wife's eyes.

Bubbles appeared, then vanished, reappeared, then vanished again. Marsh sipped his coffee and regretted his stalker-like litany. Sometimes he didn't know when to rein the hacker in. Occupational hazard.

But not a fatal one this time, far from it. Levi's reply was more than a mere detail. **I haven't slept a whole night through since she died.**

Marsh's chest clenched, recognizing Levi's lonely grief. He hadn't slept a whole night through in three years. **I get you.**

If Marsh's magenta reply had surprised Levi earlier, the reply that lit up Marsh's screen was equally unexpected and made him laugh out loud. **I hate coffee. Don't tell my Italian mother.**

The fist around his heart lightened and a hollow place there began to fill, to warm. **You're a monster.**

Wolfy: Wolfy?

Longhorn: Meet me for breakfast, and I'll tell you.

The anticoffee monster sent him the name and address of a local bakery and told him to be there in an hour.

FIVE

MARSH SPIED a suited Levi inside the corner bakery sandwiched between a Mexican eatery and a pizza joint, the tiny strip mall itself tucked deep in suburbia. Marsh suspected it was one of Levi's usual haunts, close as it was to his home. Confirmed when Marsh approached and heard Levi chatting with the older white woman behind the pastry case about her weekend. She caught sight of him over Levi's shoulder and her eyes grew wide. Round as saucers behind her cat-eye glasses when he sidled up to Levi and threw an arm over his shoulders. "What's good here, babe?"

The brim of his Stetson threatened the structural integrity of Levi's blond coif, earning him a murderous side-eye from the other agent. "Do you ever not wear the hat?"

"Do you ever not wear underwear?" The woman behind the counter giggled, and Marsh flashed her a grin. Kept it in place as he leaned closer to Levi, catching whiffs of peppermint and citrus, and whispered, "Don't answer that. We're in public, and I can't be held responsible for my actions."

"Who's your friend, Levi?" the woman asked.

Marsh removed his hat with one hand and extended the other across the case. "Emmitt Marshall. And your name, gorgeous?"

Her cheeks pinked, and she swept graying brown curls off her forehead. "Lily Lavigne. I own this place."

"Lily! That's my niece's name." He hitched his smile higher. "But she's not half as pretty as you."

Lily blushed deeper and caught herself with one hand on the counter. Mission accomplished.

"He'll have a kouign-amann and a drip coffee." Levi tried to sound irritated, but a thread of amusement twisted through his words. Marsh counted that a win too.

"Milk and sugar?" Lily asked.

"And a dash of cinnamon if you've got it," Marsh replied.

"Of course," she said with a warm smile. "Your usual, Levi?"

"Yes, please."

Levi paid for their order, then led Marsh outside to the bistro table farthest from the other customers. It was cool out, the morning marine layer heavy, but four years at The Hague had reacclimatized Marsh to dreary weather. At least here it would burn off by noon. In the meantime, his hat, flannel, and jeans would keep him toasty enough.

"If we're supposed to be engaged," Levi said, "should you be flirting with everyone in sight? And do you even like women?"

Marsh rested back in his chair, legs crossed. "Just because I'm not sexually attracted to women doesn't mean I don't love them. I was raised by two amazing women. A little harmless flirting, *if* it's welcome, makes anyone feel good." He removed his hat and rested it on his knee. "And I love to flirt almost as much as I love my Stetsons."

Levi rolled his eyes. "I'm starting to reconsider this."

"So you've considered it, then?"

"I'm consider*ing*." He turned his phone facedown on the table and straightened, his gaze sharpening. "With some ground rules."

Marsh respected the posture and the position and mirrored it himself. This was a professional proposition after all, regardless of how good Agent Bishop looked in a suit. Marsh set his hat aside and braced his forearms on the table. "I'd expect nothing less."

"This can't risk my job."

"I can't promise that."

"And I can't trust you. You fucked up my raid, Agent Marshall. Eighteen months of hard work went poof, and now we're supposed to team up? *I'm* supposed to risk *my* job when all you've demonstrated at yours so far is incompetence?" Anger gave way to apprehension, creeping across Levi's features and causing his shoulders to hitch. "Mine doesn't pay enough, but it pays and provides benefits."

Marsh could get angry at the perceived slight—it hadn't been incompetence; it had been a miscalculation—but that wouldn't get Agent Bishop on board. Humble, earnest honesty was his best shot. "I am sorry about your raid, and I understand I'm asking you to put a lot on the line. I will prove you can trust me, that I can be an asset to you on your case, and I will do everything in my power to minimize the risk to your job. As far as the Bureau will know, I'm here to visit you and check out the field office for a

possible transfer. I'll still be working my existing cases."
Levi relaxed a measure, which opened the door enough for
Marsh to ask a more probing question. "Even if you did
lose your job, would it be the worst thing in the world?
There's more than enough security and defense work in this
town. Those gigs pay better. We all know that."

"You're right, and assuming I leave the Bureau in good
standing, that's the plan, *after* I finish this case."

"Why this case?" Marsh asked, and the small progress
he'd made, to borrow Levi's words, went poof. But it
wasn't tension that rushed back in. It was the same sadness
—the lonely grief—from Friday night that colored Agent
Bishop's expression a deeper gray. Answer enough. Marsh
tentatively laid a hand over Levi's, giving it a bit more
weight when Levi didn't snatch his away. "You don't have
to tell me."

Someone cleared their throat, and Marsh glanced up.
Lily stood by their table holding a small tray, her gaze
zeroed in on their hands. "Sorry to interrupt, but I have
your food and drinks."

Marsh withdrew his hand to make room for the pastry
plates and tea and coffee service. Levi cupped his hands
around his teacup as if it were thirty degrees instead of
sixty. "Thank you, Lily."

"Yes, thank you," Marsh echoed.

She shot them another curious look, then moseyed on to
the other tables. Just as Marsh was about to switch gears
and talk strategy, Levi surprised him with an answer to his
last question. "Kristin brought me this case. She was doing
pro bono work with asylum seekers when one of them went
missing."

Marsh had suspected Levi's late wife's involvement. His

commitment to the case was personal. "The client was trafficked?"

"By someone who offered her money, education, and a life in exchange for marriage."

A too common story with trafficked victims. The criminals preyed on the hopeless, offered money, success, education, sex, love, stability, any number of lures to draw a person into an even more hopeless situation. "Have you found her?"

Levi shook his head, then bit into his chocolate croissant.

"We will," Marsh said.

"If she's even still alive…"

It was a fact they had to acknowledge with any missing persons case and especially with trafficked victims. A fact Marsh had had to learn decades ago when soldiers didn't return to camp, like he'd seen time and again in his legat work.

"Try the pastry," Levi said with a jut of his chin at the round laminated pastry on Marsh's plate.

It was formed like a cinnamon roll, a pinwheel of pastry sheets spinning inward. Seeing no easy way to break off a piece, Marsh bit into one side… and groaned at the explosion of flavors across his tongue. Not as sweet as a cinnamon roll and denser than a croissant with flaky layers of pastry basted in butter, sugar, and vanilla. "This is amazing."

Levi smiled, the first full one Marsh had drawn from him that morning. Marsh counted it another victory. "Everything here is," Levi said, "but those are the best in town." They finished eating in comfortable silence, Levi checking his phone twice more.

Once Lily cleared their plates, Marsh circled back to the plan he was proposing and how to execute it. "I'll need to move in to sell this."

Levi didn't immediately object, a good sign, until he backtracked farther. "Why is anyone going to believe this, including our targets? Do we *want* them to notice? Should we be broadcasting this?"

Good questions. Levi had been considering—all the angles. So had Marsh in the hours of sleep he wasn't getting. "Yes, we want them to notice, and yes, there is some danger in that."

"There's danger every day we go to work and every day we investigate any aspect of this operation. I'd personally rather have *all* the info and know *all* the players and threats, which you're telling me there are more of now."

"That's right, and that's what I'm trying to get at. The ultimate goal here is to apply pressure so the money, the higher-ups, tip their hands. We can keep chasing traffickers and terrorists or"—he snapped a limb off a withered bush in the curbside planter—"we can cut off the money that keeps them going. That's what I was trying to do last week. Pressure the larger organization into making a move, only they made a different one, which again, I apologize for. It was a miscalculation on my part."

"And us married won't be another miscalculation? How does that even fit into your apply pressure plan?"

Marsh held up a finger. "I'll get there, but first, are you familiar with chess?"

"Vaguely. Kristin was good at it, taught David, but it was never my thing."

"In chess terms, you could say we're both at a dead draw with our respective cases. No player has a chance of winning." In their lives too, but the way Levi was darkly eyeing him over the rim of his teacup, Marsh didn't go there.

"That's ominous," Levi said.

"Which is why a theoretical novelty is needed."

"A what?"

"An opening move that's not been played before."

Levi gestured between them. "Us married."

"Exactly. We're not undercover pretending to be married. It's not essential to the case itself, but we've got a better shot at solving our cases, at bringing down the entire empire, together, with an open channel of communication and with all the information. And since the Bureau's not going to let us do that officially…"

"Us married."

Marsh withdrew his phone, opened an encrypted file, and placed it on the table in front of Levi. "After a whirl-wind romance that, if anyone looks, is well documented."

Levi set aside his cup, picked up the phone, and swiped his finger over the screen, scrolling through the meticu-lously curated collection of pictures, receipts, airline tickets, and more, his mouth gaping wider with each piece of manufactured evidence. "How?"

"Hacker," Marsh reminded. "Also tight with other hack-ers. Our employer and our enemies *will* buy this if *we* sell it."

Levi returned the phone, then sank back in his chair, legs and arms crossed, considering. After a nerve-racking minute, he returned to the spot Marsh had brought them to earlier and moved a square forward. "We have the extra room at the house."

Marsh navigated carefully, not wanting to jeopardize the

progress made but also locating all the pieces on the board. "And David?"

"Knows this isn't real. He's the one who told me to do it. For the money."

Surprising and yet not. After Marsh's father had left, he and his mother had become an even tighter unit than they'd already been. No secrets, no lies, just honest conversations. Money hadn't been a concern, the divorce settlement more than sufficient, but they'd checked in regularly about where their lives were headed. He suspected Levi and David had a similar relationship, even if they'd arrived at it differently. "And the rest of your family?"

"My oldest sister knows. We'll have to sell this to the rest of them and to the extended family at a wedding later this month."

Marsh grinned as he guzzled his coffee. "Sounds like fun."

"You can flirt, but don't touch. That goes for as long as we're married. And you better be ready to explain to my mother why she wasn't invited to the wedding."

"No problem on the first." As if Marsh could even look at another man like that when Levi was in the same room, when his ring was on Marsh's finger, for real or not. But that was him. Their cover had to work both ways. "As long as the same goes for you."

"Of course."

Marsh stifled the satisfied sigh that wanted to escape. "As for your mother, she can come to the courthouse."

"I won't put her through that, not for something that's not real. I've already broken her heart once."

Marsh would've lurched across the table and shaken the man—then hugged the daylights out of him—if they weren't in public. He settled for clasping Levi's forearm tight enough to draw his gaze. "Kristin dying was not your fault."

Levi's blue gaze bounced away. "Maybe if I'd been home more, I would've noticed she was sick."

"And what would she say to that?"

"That I was being ridiculous."

"You're being ridiculous," Marsh repeated in her stead. Levi's gaze drifted back to him, and the accompanying smile was soft and way too fucking attractive. Marsh retreated before he lurched across the table for a different reason. "Any other ground rules?"

"We keep this professional." Exactly the ground rule Marsh needed to hear as he fantasized about what Levi's soft smile might look like after—"I don't have time for a new relationship. My attention needs to be on this case and on David."

Fair, except... "What about time for yourself?" Levi's tired, bitter laugh cut right to Marsh's heart. Alrighty, then, time to start taking care of his husband, for purely professional reasons of course. Marsh held out his hand. "Give me your phone."

"Why?"

"So I can program in the rest of my numbers."

Levi handed him the device. "How many more are there?"

Distraction apprehended, Marsh stood.

"Wait!" Levi shot to the end of his chair, feet planted apart, moving to stand. "Where are you going? And you never told me why I'm Wolfy."

Marsh clasped his shoulder, forestalling his upward momentum and thrilled in a decidedly unprofessional manner at Levi's muffled gasp, at the streaks of red that colored his impressive cheekbones. The growl Marsh struggled to repress came out like gravel around his words. "To get a box of those pastries to go, and you'll have to wait on the other." He flipped his hat back onto his head and pointed at the half-full cup of tea in front of Levi. "For now, you're going to take five minutes to enjoy your peppermint leaf water."

"I don't need—"

"Yes, you do."

Before Marsh could fully pivot, Levi grasped his wrist, the hold delightfully, dangerously strong. "Do *you* have any ground rules?"

Against his better judgment, Marsh stepped between Levi's spread knees, forcing his gaze up. "One, don't lie to me. I'm your partner now. I'm also a soldier. I will have your back, and I won't leave you behind." Levi's rosier blush and his quickened breaths were appealing, but the revived spark of confidence in his eyes was fucking captivating. Marsh preened. He liked being the one who gave Levi the security he needed to get some of that moxie back.

"And two?" Levi prompted.

"Same as yours. We keep this professional."

"What's your excuse?" And oh, if Marsh had thought Levi's soft smile was attractive, his cocky smirk was all kinds of sinful.

Marsh leaned down, the shadow of his hat eclipsing Levi's upturned face, and inhaled deep, another lungful of Levi's fresh citrusy scent. Fuck, everything about him was enticing. "If I'm your type, you're mine, dangerously so, and neither of us can afford to lose sight of what matters here."

Levi's gaze remained locked with his. "The case."

Yes, the case. The professional straw they were both desperately grasping at. The endgame that had to matter more than what either of them personally may come to want.

SIX

"ALL RIGHT, SO, WHERE ARE WE?" Levi stood at the head of the conference table in his team's war room. Over a year's worth of boxes were stacked in the corners, the white board at one end of the room was full of scribbled notes and photos, legal pads, pens, and folders littered the table, and the coffee pot at the other end of the room ran perpetually low. Special Agents Matthew Kim, Alyssa Meyers, and Will Dawson sat around the table, each with a half cup of coffee or less and a laptop in front of them. "Assuming our traffickers change the next transfer point, do we have leads on when or where that'll be now?"

"We think it's already gone down." Matt, a New Yorker by way of the Boston field office, pushed a stack of photos in front of him. "Surveillance footage from a truck stop outside Albuquerque. They haven't used this one before. We didn't have eyes on. Footage came in from a missing persons contact I have down there."

Levi spread out the grainy photos. The repurposed moving truck was the exact right size—big enough to cram ten or so people behind boxes, small enough to avoid weigh stations—and the man hauling women out of the back of the truck and shuttling them into separate SUVs was familiar too. No positive ID on him—he was always careful to avoid cameras, careful to always operate outside their jurisdiction—but his size and build, the ink on his forearms, and his presence at all the transfers were enough to identify him as a repeat player. "How many victims?"

"Eight to ten," Alyssa replied.

Consistent with their preraid intel. "Do we know the victims' destinations?"

Will, the most junior agent on their team, shook his head. "Unmarked truck, no manifests. Couldn't get plates on the SUVs. Likely headed for casinos in Nevada or the Ozarks." And then where, after they outlasted their usefulness as underpaid waitresses for the gamblers and pit bosses to grope?

"Fuck." Levi pushed off the table. Out of their jurisdiction either way. He paced the length of the room, hands laced behind his head. "Will, notify the other task force teams, particularly those in Nevada and along the I-40 corridor."

"On it." He spun in his chair and scrambled out of the room, headed for his bullpen desk.

"Do we have any leads on the next exchange?" Levi asked.

"Nothing solid," Matt replied. "Working contacts and checking manifests and missing persons reports." Agent Kim's missing persons work in Boston brought a valuable skillset and list of contacts to the trafficking task force.

"All right, we regroup and intercept the next exchange."

"In who knows how long," Alyssa said with a heavy

sigh. She'd been on this case as long as Levi and was just as frustrated. "Could be months like last time."

"Not likely."

Alyssa and Matt spun the direction of the unfamiliar voice. Levi was used to it enough by now not to startle, which probably made his jolt when he did look up all the more amusing to the man in the doorway. Gone were Marsh's worn jeans, flannel, and tee. Gone was the white Stetson. In their place was a sleek black version of the hat, a designer sports coat, a crisp white button-down, and dress slacks that had to be tailored to fit so well. If he'd thought Mount Cowboy was handsome before, this new look was more than Levi could handle on only three cups of tea. Judging by Marsh's smirk, the asshole knew it, but he had the good grace to focus on the case instead as they'd agreed earlier that morning. "The payment was too much for one transport," he said.

"Who are you?" Alyssa asked.

"Special Agent Emmitt Marshall." He tossed two file folders onto the table, then extended a hand to Alyssa. "I'm a visiting cyber agent."

"You here to help, Agent Marshall?" Matt said as they shook hands next. "My old partner is tight with a former cyber agent. You hackers can work magic." Lucky for Marsh, the rest of Levi's team didn't know it was him who'd interfered last week. That information had stayed between Levi and the higher-ups. And Marsh had more broadly labeled himself as a cyber agent, not a cyber legat.

"Marsh, please." Done with introductions, he crossed the room to Levi's side and flashed him a grin. "And if by *help*, you mean marrying this grumpy bastard, then yes."

Will squeaked from the doorway while Alyssa gasped a "What?" and Matt a "Married?"

Levi split a glance between Will and Alyssa first. "Give us the room, please. I need to bring Agent Kim up to speed, then we'll brief you." Matt, the other senior agent on the case, also reported directly to Levi's ASAC and the task force AD. More than that, he was one of the sharpest agents Levi had ever worked with. This would be his and Marsh's first test at selling their cover. Matt needed to buy it, and Marsh needed to stay in Matt's good graces if they had any hope of making the charade work.

Levi shut the door behind the other agents as Matt leaned a hip against the table. "I know I haven't been here long, but I thought we were friends. I thought…"

"I asked him to keep it quiet," Marsh said. He plucked the file folders off the table, handing one to Levi. He flipped through the stack of disclosures as Marsh continued to explain to Matt. "We need to talk to your ASAC and make the appropriate disclosures." He offered the other file folder to Matt. "A peace offering. It's what I could pull together on those jewel thieves you're looking into."

Matt riffled through the file. "But this isn't official."

"Professional courtesy. Wanted to make a good impression on my fiancé's team."

Matt snapped shut the file, and despite the setback on their case, he looked energized, his dark eyes glittering. "Thank you for this. You helping out on our case too?"

"That one's all you guys." Marsh returned to Levi's side and slid a big warm hand into the groove at his lower back. Levi barely suppressed his shiver. Marsh's rumbly voice didn't help. "We're supposed to meet with the ASAC in five."

"Go," Matt said. "I'll catch Alyssa and Will up." He shooed them toward the door with the file. "And thanks again for this."

They were halfway across the bullpen when Levi whispered low, "Well played with the assist."

"I wasn't sure how many people knew I blew the last op."

"Only me and the bosses but good to get Matt on our side in case he does find out. Whatcha got up your sleeve for the ASAC? 'That fucking cowboy' is her new favorite phrase."

"Heard it before." Smiling, Marsh snagged a familiar box of baked goods off an empty bullpen desk. "Little bit of sugar should do the trick."

♟♟♝♜♛♚♝♟♟

MARSH FOLLOWED Levi into the ASAC's corner office, and a wave of quiet comfort washed over him. The figure standing in profile by the windows had changed her work attire—traded her fatigues for a sharp burgundy suit—but her military bearing was unmistakable as was her thick black hair gathered into a low bun and the delicate features that had fooled countless combatants into thinking she was an easy target. They couldn't have been more wrong. Her call sign was a far more accurate representation of the strength, will, and intelligence bundled into a deceptively petite package.

"Eagle," Marsh said, beating Levi to an unnecessary introduction.

"Nerd." Major Julia Kwan turned from the window, face

a blank mask Marsh couldn't read. While she'd taken Brax's calls over the weekend, she'd ignored all Marsh's attempts. He hoped she was the same soldier she used to be, that she would understand what he'd done and what he was doing. "Imagine my surprise when Colonel Marshall appeared on my calendar today."

"Colonel?" Levi's head swiveled, his gaze darting between him and Kwan. Marsh could have warned him that he and Kwan shared a past, but there'd been little time between convincing Levi to play ball and securing their cover. Plus, he liked keeping Levi on his toes.

"That's the rank I retired with. Major was hers." He nodded Kwan's direction. "And she's the one who roped me into this FBI gig." He slid the box of pastries onto her desk. "Thought it was time I stopped by to say thanks."

She eyed the box as she circled the desk. "Is that what you're doing? Because I thought you were here to fucking cowboy up the place. I'll need to find my spurs again to keep you in line."

She sounded menacing, but affection belied the hard-ass projection. Thank fuck. Could've gone either way. He opened his arms, and Kwan stepped into them. "I missed you, Nerd."

"Missed you too, Eagle." Over her shoulder, he spied the wooden chess box he'd given her as a thank you gift for introducing him to Sophie and the FBI. "Been practicing your chess game?"

"When I can, though no one's as good a teacher as you."

"Wait!" Levi squawked behind them. "So you two *do* know each other? The way you cursed him out the other night I thought maybe you did, but I figured it was another op he'd fucked up."

Marsh scoffed over his shoulder. "Hey!"

Kwan's snicker didn't make him feel any better. He shifted to Kwan's side, an arm thrown over her shoulders. "This one made a habit out of busting my balls in the desert."

"Someone had to rein your cowboy ass in, especially after Kane retired." She slipped out from under his arm and peeked into the pastry box. Same ole sweet tooth. "He sounded good when I talked to him this weekend."

"Disgustingly happy. Shacked up with Madigan officially."

"We all knew that would happen." Pastry in hand, she retreated behind her desk and sank into her chair. "Took 'em long enough."

"So you two were in the army together?" Levi asked him as they slid into the visitor chairs across from Kwan. "And why didn't you tell me before we walked in here?"

"Stationed together in Afghanistan. She discharged before me, and I didn't tell you so I could see that look on your face."

"Not amused."

Kwan laughed around a bite. "You're not the first person to say that about him. Unfortunate side effect."

Marsh scoffed her direction this time. "Hey!"

She shrugged. "He's good at what he does, most of the time, which was why, when I was with the Bureau's terrorism task force and we lost a target in the desert, I roped him in for cyber and operational support."

"That's when I got hooked up with Sophie and the legat program," Marsh explained, trying to keep his voice light and knowing he'd failed when Kwan's smile dimmed.

She reached across her desk, hand offered. Marsh

slipped his into hers, and she squeezed. "She was a good agent."

"Hell of a friend and mentor too. Transition to civilian life would've been a lot harder without her and Sean."

Kwan withdrew her hand and snagged another pastry. "That's why you're after the money? You think your terrorists are somehow connected to Agent Bishop's traffickers."

He nodded.

"And you're here now to what? Weasel your way back onto the case? Because I can tell you right now, from on high, that's not gonna happen."

"No, I'm here to marry him."

Kwan froze, pastry halfway to her mouth. "I'm sorry, what?"

"Levi and I are engaged."

She tossed the pastry aside, wiped off her hands, then folded them on the desk, all congeniality gone, one hundred percent the ASAC. "Break that shit down, *Barney* style." With a side of scary desert ballbuster. Guess she'd found those spurs.

She'd buy this particular bullshit better from Levi. Marsh shifted in his chair, angling his fiancé's direction, and his heart dropped. Levi was simmering, his eyes a steely, battered blue and the divot between them a canyon. Wolfy was angry. So not telling him had been another miscalculation. But Marsh's plan was not. He channeled every bit of pleading into his gaze, begging Levi to play his part.

The two seconds of silence that followed were the longest of Marsh's life. He prayed he hadn't botched this mission already. Finally, Levi swung his attention to Kwan, scooted to the end of his chair, and handed her the folder of disclosures. "We met last December when I was in San Francisco on the Boggs case."

Marsh blew his sigh of relief out through his nostrils, muffling it as best he could. "I was in town visiting Brax. Swung by the office to introduce myself to the SAC there since I'd heard so much about him. Even the Irishman's good looks couldn't distract me from the blond bombshell striding across the bullpen floor." It wasn't exactly the truth —their paths hadn't crossed in the office—but if they had, Marsh knew which direction he would've been looking. At the agent now beside him fighting a grin. "Said to myself right then I was going to marry him."

Levi's smile escaped, along with the rosy blush Marsh couldn't get enough of. Made him wonder if the rest of Levi's body flushed the same way when he—

"So you've been dating since December?" Kwan said, popping the fantasy bubble. "And you're just now disclosing in June?"

"We weren't sure if it would go anywhere," Marsh replied. "With me being overseas."

"This paperwork says you're considering a transfer."

"Or the private sector. Whatever gets me to San Diego and him."

"It would be a shame for the Bureau to lose you." Dark brows pinched, she was in a bind.

Marsh had put her there, they both knew it, so he played his hand harder. Damage was already done. "Then signing that paperwork shouldn't be a problem."

Her brows pinched tighter. "Good initiative, bad judgment."

"TBD."

"You know I don't believe this shit for a second."

"You don't have to believe it," Marsh said. "You just have to sign off on the disclosures."

She pushed out of her chair with a huff. "You were a good soldier. One of the best cybers Camp Casey ever saw. And you're a good agent by all accounts. But I cannot have your cowboy shit turning this office or my agents upside down. We're on a short leash."

"What does that mean?"

"It means I'm a woman of color working under a man who would rather smoke cigars and sip whiskey than do his job. And I'm okay with that because the more time he spends at the club, the more we get done. The more lives we save and people we protect. That's why I'm here. That's why Agent Bishop is here." She braced her hands on the desk, staring him down. "We do not need you fucking things up."

He lifted his hands, palms out. "You won't even know I'm here."

Her unamused laugh pinged off the windows and unadorned walls, only a case with her flag and medals over the credenza. She directed her chagrin at Levi. "You're on board with this?"

"I said yes."

To any trained investigator, it was a qualified *yes* at best.

"Let me be clear." Kwan straightened and snatched a pen off her desk. "My priority is this office and the mission. If you two get caught, I can't protect you."

"And if we catch your target and mine?" Marsh said.

"I didn't hear that." She flipped open the folder and signed where Marsh had flagged. "You've met with your team, Agent Bishop? They have orders?"

"Yes, ma'am."

"Then get out of here for the rest of the afternoon." She threw her pen down, picked up the folder, and circled the desk. She stopped in front of Levi and shoved the folder at him. "Think real hard about whether you want to turn this into HR tomorrow."

"Ma'am—"

Kwan shut him up with a raised hand. "I need time to wrap my own head around this."

Levi nodded and turned toward the door. Marsh moved to follow, but Kwan stopped him with a hand around his biceps. When he looked back, it wasn't only the San Diego field office ASAC staring at him; it was his friend, his colleague, his fellow soldier. "Watch his six."

Marsh raised his hand in a salute. "Roger that, Major."

SEVEN

"THIS IS YOUR HOTEL ROOM?" Levi made a slow circuit around the spacious room with its elegant furnishings, high-end electronics, and marble bathroom, winding up where his gaze had first been drawn to, in front of the balcony doors with their unobstructed views of the Pacific. "Do I even want to know how much a night here costs?"

Behind him, Marsh moved around the room, pulling bags from the closet and clothes out of drawers. "It's just a hotel room. It has its limitations."

"What limitations?" There was a fully stocked kitchenette in one corner, a king-size bed under a mountain of pillows, a café table between two club chairs, an executive desk with an ocean view, and a safe in the bottom half of the bedside table that Marsh was removing case files and laptops from.

"Fine. I found a room with a view that had everything I needed for an extended stay. I was here the night of the raid, and I was going to stay here if you didn't agree to marry me."

"You were still going to investigate?"

"Yes." He retrieved a toiletry bag from the bathroom and a portable chess set from the desk drawer, shoving both into one of the two duffels on the bed. "And even if you did agree, I wasn't sure if you'd want to work at your house or if we could at the office, so…"

He gestured around the room, and while Levi appreciated the consideration, he couldn't escape the feeling that the world was spinning way too fast around him. The same feeling that had sent him reeling at the office, watching Marsh and Kwan embrace and banter like the old friends they were. Spinning faster when Marsh had pushed her to the edge of her patience.

He sank onto the end of the bed before his legs gave out from under him. "What happened to ground rule number one?"

"Kwan will work with us."

"That's not what it sounded like to me."

"Well, she won't work against us. I've known that woman more than fifteen years. All that matters to her is the mission. As long as we don't fuck that up, she'll look the other way."

Levi shot to his feet, rounding the corner of the bed and bearing down on Marsh. "You've already fucked up the mission!" Hating the strangled, desperate frustration in his voice, he spun away just as quickly. He stopped in front of the balcony doors, white-knuckling the wooden frame as he stared out at the ocean. The waves usually calmed him, reminded him of his parents' place, of a simpler time, but everything in the present was so damn topsy-turvy. His job and case up in the air, his son walking the surly teen tightrope, the unwanted attraction and simmering anger he swung between in Agent Marshall's presence. He couldn't see out of the big tent long enough to catch any comforting memories. He'd always hated the fucking circus. "I can't lose this job, Marsh. You probably don't understand if you can afford a hotel room like this, but—"

A check appeared on the desk in Levi's periphery, and Levi choked on his words. He hadn't seen that many zeros in... he couldn't remember when. Maybe not ever.

"Does that make you feel better?" Marsh's warm breath tickled Levi's nape, his tea tree oil scent Levi's nose, the heat from his big body every inch of Levi's even though they weren't touching.

Levi focused on the ginormous check and not the temptation behind him. "You can just cut a check for that amount?"

"I need to call the bank to authorize it, but yes. I'd appreciate if you'd wait until after our wedding and after we've opened a joint account to deposit it so the money is considered community property. That's the other part of why we need to be married. So this money isn't taxed as a gift. I know what I'm asking. I want to make sure you get every cent of this in return."

"What if this whole arrangement goes bust in a week?"

"What if it works, and we solve our cases in a week?" He pushed the check more squarely into Levi's line of sight. "It's insurance, breathing room from your creditors, and peace of mind."

The tilt-a-whirl spun faster, the past seventy-two hours crashing into Levi all at once. "I can't... I can't take that."

"Yes, you can because I'm asking you to take this." An open ring box appeared on top of the check. Two matching bands nestled in dark velvet.

Levi plucked free one of the rings and examined the work of art, a geometric design hammered into the platinum strip inlaid in a band of rose gold. "This is beautiful."

Marsh gently cradled his hand and turned it so the ring caught the sunlight streaming in through the balcony doors. "It's from one of the local artisans near the ranch. Mom's wife takes care of his menagerie of pets, and he pays her in jewelry."

"I can't—"

Marsh closed his fingers over Levi's and tugged him the rest of the way around, their hands clasped between them. "You can, Levi. If you can help me with this case, then I can help you. Let me, please."

Staring into Marsh's dark, determined eyes, feeling the band of sun-warmed metal between their palms, the even warmer body close to his, closer than anyone had been in months, Levi took a chance, nodded, and his world finally stopped spinning.

♟♟♜♚♚♚♚♛♟♟

MARSH DIDN'T EXPECT Levi's acceptance of his not-a-real proposal to knock him for a loop, to feel as real as it did, but holding Levi close, a ring between them, with Levi's wary yet hopeful blues locked with his, packed more of a punch than Marsh had bargained for. Made resisting the urge to dip his head and kiss the daylights out of the other agent almost impossible.

Other *agent*.

He did resist. Barely.

Leaving the ring in Levi's hand, Marsh withdrew and

returned to the laptops on the bed. He snagged his personal one and opened it on the desk. "We've got a few minutes," he said as he booted up the computer and navigated his multiple layers of security. "Let me show you what I've got."

Levi seemed relieved by the change of subject. He tucked the ring back into its case and circled the desk to stand beside Marsh. "Is this what you mentioned to Matt and the team?" He jutted a chin at the files Marsh was opening on-screen. "About the money being too much for one transport?"

Marsh nodded. "My legat team specialized in transnational organized crime. Three years ago, we were investigating a human trafficking operation in Europe." He pointed at the first spreadsheet. "These are the accounts and transactions we identified as associated with the operation. Similar overpayment pattern. The traffickers weren't paid for each transport but for multiple transports at a time." He brought forward the PDF of the wire confirmation he'd found the day of the Vienna bombing. "This was a deposit made to a Balkan-based ISIS cell three days before the bombing in Vienna that killed Sophie."

Levi leaned closer and peered at the screen. "Same bank, and the account numbers are close."

Marsh maximized the third file, an account ledger. "This is the account that wired money to *your* traffickers."

Levi straightened, tilted his head, and with his blue eyes catching the sun, Marsh couldn't help but think of a curious wolf. "That's not the same bank as the first two."

"Correct, but—"

"Same transaction behavior." Sharp as a wolf too.

"Which is why I submitted a warrant and pulled the

account control agreements. Got the names of the account holders. I did some digging, and these are the corporate org charts. The entity that funded your traffickers in San Diego and the entities that funded traffickers and suicide bombers in Europe." He opened the charts on the computer screen. "See the pattern?"

"Layers and layers of subsidiaries that all lead back to this company in Vienna." He tapped the screen with a fingertip, and the computer nerd in Marsh barely resisted the urge to slap it down. "Eder Capital."

"Want to know where else EC invests?" Marsh opened the interactive map he'd been building the past three years. Red dots of varying sizes appeared in the Balkans, Belarus, Syria, Mexico, Thailand, and the Central African Republic.

"Where are they in the US?" Levi asked.

Marsh scrolled left to the Americas and more dots appeared on-screen. "DC, Nevada, California, and Missouri." Three of those locations were among the top five trafficking risk areas in the States.

Levi's mouth opened and closed several times, questions no doubt flying as the investigator's brain made connections. He finally settled on the most obvious query. "Why haven't you gone after Eder before?"

"We tried, but this is a sophisticated operation. EC is well insulated by lawyers and corporate structures, and their funds flow is structured to look like donations, infrastructure projects, and casinos that are touted as efforts to revitalize local economies. They've got more politicians in their pockets than those yahoos out of Kansas could ever hope for. To most of the world, Eder Capital looks like a group of philanthropic venture capitalists promoting enlightened capitalism worldwide." He maximized the last file he'd opened. "This is the path of just one of those payments."

Ten million dollars traveled a circuitous route around the globe and ended right back in EC's account—as thirty million dollars.

Levi scoffed. "They're not philanthropists. They're fucking money launderers."

"That's the generous interpretation. They're murderers taking their cut from the terrorists and traffickers—human, organ, arms, drugs, you name it—they do business with."

"Jesus." Levi backed away from the desk, clasped his hands behind his head, and paced the longest part of the room from the entry door to the balcony door. Marsh recalled the day he'd put it all together—that tangled rush of revelation, frustration, and excitement. Now all that lingered was frustration, hence the drastic maneuver in the velvet box still sitting on the other end of the desk. He waited for Levi to burn the rush out and return to his side. Once there, Levi pointed at the western half of the map. "This was the route we were working for the traffickers." He traced a path from Mexico to San Diego, then two branches, one north to Nevada and the other east to Chicago via Missouri. "Nevada and Missouri are the usual destinations, but sometimes they transport victims as far as Chicago. We've been using funds flow, cargo manifests, and missing person reports."

"Then that's where we start." Marsh closed the laptop and rocked back in his chair. "We try to get ahead of the next transport."

"So we're after the facilitator, then?" Facilitators were the middlemen, connecting capital to criminals.

"Nailing the facilitator is phase two on our way to ultimately nailing EC."

Levi rested against the edge of the desk. "And phase one?"

"Disrupting operations here in the States so badly that their source of funds and their supply chain, as awful as I know that sounds, are compromised. The facilitator, or better yet, EC, will have to show their hand."

"That's what you were trying to do last weekend." The usual anger in Levi's voice about the botched raid had morphed into understanding, a welcome change.

Marsh nodded as he stood. "They moved the transport up. That part worked. The last-minute location change was the miscalculation. And there was a missing minute in the security feed I should have spotted when their man waiting on-site abandoned ship. In any event, the idea is to exert enough stress on the foundation of the operation that they'll have to poke their heads out to take action. We keep this next operation locked down—need to know only, and I go about things more carefully—so your traffickers don't have time to make adjustments, then EC will have even fewer options." He counted them off on his fingers. "Deterrence, retribution, or soliciting new clients."

One corner of Levi's mouth hitched. "And that's when we catch them."

Marsh smirked to match. "And that's when we catch them."

It felt good to have a partner again. Someone to strategize with, to bounce ideas off, to celebrate the wins and mourn the losses in what would be a guerrilla effort. Had been so far. The welcome camaraderie sank into Marsh's bones, reminded him just how long he'd been going at it alone, propelled him closer to the source of that companionship.

Beside him, Levi inched closer and tilted his head. His eyelids fluttered closed, dark blond lashes on pale cheeks, and a breath escaped his lips, ghosting over Marsh's, drawing him the rest of the way—

A phone alarm trilled, startling them apart, Levi reversing hard and fast. "What's that?"

"Our reminder."

"Reminder for what?" His voice trembled as he ran a shaky hand through his hair.

Marsh didn't think his answer would help those ripples of banked desire, the same ones coursing through Marsh, but it was now or never. He snatched up the ring box. "Time to *I do*."

EIGHT

LEVI LOWERED the phone from his ear and disconnected the unanswered call, not bothering with a voicemail after the other three he'd left already. "I can't get David to pick up."

Marsh parked the Bureau cruiser in the county administration building's parking lot. "Our appointment is in ten minutes. Even if he picked up now, could he get here in time?"

"Fuck." Levi dropped the phone into his lap and slumped in his seat. Eyes closed, he scrubbed a hand over his face, mentally cursing the too swiftly moving clock and also Marsh for not giving him enough heads-up. "I can't get married without my son there."

"Is this about David or about his mother?"

There was that too. In Marsh's hotel room, Levi had let the *this better not fuck up my job* talk and the *this cowboy is smarter than I gave him credit for* feelings distract him from the hardest part of the entire scenario. The guilt that had started as a dull ache in the pit of his stomach and intensified as they'd neared the waterfront now sat like an elephant on his chest as he eyed the distinctive government building through the windshield. He rubbed at the wretched pain with his fist. "It feels like a betrayal."

Marsh gently grasped his wrist and drew his hand down, holding it lightly on the console between their seats. "You have nothing to feel guilty about. Yes, this is a legal marriage, but your heart hasn't betrayed Kristin. But, Levi..." Marsh's gentle tug drew Levi's gaze. "One day you *will* fall in love again, and that won't be a betrayal either. From what I've gathered about Kristin, she'd want that for you."

He nodded, remembering those final days in hospice and the muted conversations he and Kristin had shared during her more lucid moments. Recalling the lectures—no, *adjustments*—she'd given him because she knew him better than he did himself. "She made me promise her." Tears escaped as he forced words out around the lump in his throat. "She didn't have the strength to eat or drink, could barely even move, but she squeezed my hand and made me promise to look love in the face again one day."

Marsh squeezed the same hand his late wife had, a connection bridging past and present. "You can do this, Levi, but only if you want to. We can call this whole thing off. It's your play."

He withdrew his hand and swiped at the wet on his cheeks. "She'd also tell me to do whatever it takes to solve this case."

"All right, then, let's do this." Marsh cranked the car long enough to roll up the windows, then reached into the backseat to grab the white hat he'd swapped for the black one.

Levi glanced once more at his phone. "I just wish…"

"Wouldn't you rather David be there when you're ready to look love in the face again and say I do?" He settled a big warm hand on Levi's shoulder. "He should see how brave his father is to take that chance."

Fuck, he was too perfect. Levi wanted to lean across the console and kiss him and wasn't that a complete and total mindfuck after the conversation they'd just had. "Jesus."

Marsh smirked as if he had a front row seat to Levi's mental gymnastics. "Haven't we covered this?"

Levi shook his head, bemused. "Amy's gonna love you."

He wasn't wrong.

Inside, they rounded the corner to the clerk's office and Levi spied Amy at the end of the hall, chatting with a tall spindly man Levi recognized as Braxton Kane. As soon as she caught sight of them, she stopped midconversation and made a slow sweep of the man beside Levi from his polished boots to his bright white hat. Her dark eyes widened, and her mouth rounded into an O.

"You must be Amy," Marsh said as they approached. Levi had been around him enough now to notice how he modulated his voice, laying the accent on thicker when he wanted to charm or distract. "Emmitt Marshall," he said. "Pleased to meet you."

"Don't let the syrup fool you," Brax said, wise to Marsh's ways.

"Zip it, Brooklyn," Marsh said with a zipping motion of his fingers and a spot-on impression of Brax's New York accent.

Amy tore her gaze from the cowboy long enough to cast Levi a devilish grin. "I don't care how this came about"—

she gestured between the two of them—"Aunt Liz is gonna shit."

Levi laughed out loud, the elephant from earlier traipsing off for now, its weight lifting off his chest. "Marsh, my sister, Amy Bishop."

"I like you," Marsh said to her, then clasped Brax's shoulder. "Better than I like this one."

Brax scoffed around a crooked smile. "Get over here, asshole." Marsh's faux affront melted, and the two men embraced, their hug tight and lingering. Something else Levi had noticed about Marsh—despite his swagger, there was a vibrating tension about him, a mental chess game always running behind his dark eyes. He expended so much energy being *the* Emmitt Marshall, but in Brax's arms, Marsh let the front drop, his big body relaxing, his smile stretching into something easy and true.

It was a sight to behold. One that made Levi insanely, irrationally jealous. He wanted to be that person for Marsh.

Marsh leaned back and clasped Brax's shoulders. "Thank you for being here."

"Wasn't gonna miss this. Holt sends his regards. Toddler emergency."

"Aww, you could have brought the princess with you." He flicked the brim of his cap. "New hat for her to destroy."

"Next time, I promise."

Levi snapped out of the green-hued fog when Amy whispered in his ear, "If I wasn't a lesbian, I would let that cowboy ride me all night long." She snickered at his answering splutter.

"Bishop-Marshall party," the clerk called from the office behind them, saving Levi from further embarrassment. At least for the next twenty minutes while he and Marsh filled out the necessary paperwork. The clerk only once gave them a sideways glance when they both presented their FBI badges as a second form of government-issued ID. Marsh unfurled his honeyed-accent, assured her she wouldn't get in trouble for marrying them, and once that media-induced hiccup was overcome, their group followed the clerk out of the building.

"How did you manage an appointment on such short notice?" Levi asked as they made their way down to the arbor by the water. "Given her reaction to our badges, I don't think you played the FBI card."

"Different badge, so to speak. This is a military town. Your family served, I served, there's always someone who knows someone, even across branch—"

His words and steps faltered, and Levi nearly stumbled beside him. "Marsh?" When that didn't garner a response, he gave his shoulder a nudge and said his name again. Still nothing.

Was *Marsh* getting cold feet? *Now*?

Levi glanced from Marsh to the arbor where the clerk and their friends moved into position beneath the arch of flowers.

The flowers.

Bougainvillea.

Levi couldn't stop the grin from splitting his face. "You didn't look at pictures before you booked the appointment?"

Marsh removed his hat, held it over his chest, and shook his head. His expression of wonder and peace, a dash of that same easiness from earlier when he'd embraced Brax, was a lovely sight.

His hand curling around Levi's was an even lovelier feeling.

"There a problem, Major Marshall?" Brax called.

"I thought you were a colonel?" Levi said.

Marsh cleared his throat but didn't take back his hand. "Wrong titles are a thing with him and Holt." His gaze, though, remained locked on the arbor that bloomed with the magenta flowers he loved. "If I believed in fate…"

"Don't most cowboys?"

Marsh swung his gaze to Levi and his rich brown eyes were full of something Levi couldn't put words to. Was afraid to. "If you're not careful, Agent Bishop, this one might start to."

MARSH RESTED against the harbor railing and watched as Amy laughed at something Levi said, the two of them seated on a stone bench near the arbor. Heads close, it was impossible not to notice the sibling resemblance—same high cheekbones, same straight noses, mismatched lips that stretched into balanced smiles, a shared spark of mischief in their eyes. Those two would be trouble—the good kind.

"When we talked Thursday night, I don't recall 'marry Agent Bishop' being on the list of ways to get back into Kwan's good graces."

"Friday morning, technically." Marsh tore his gaze from the Bishops and gave his attention to the man who'd hopped a same-day flight for him. "Thanks for getting down here so fast."

"My business partner has a private jet at her disposal."

"How is the bounty hunter business going?"

"Well." Brax shifted, blocking Levi and Amy from Marsh's wandering gaze. "Now quit dodging."

Damn cop, always with the interrogations. "I took the evidence Holt helped me gather and put it to good use. Beyond that, it's better if you don't know. Plausible deniability and all that shit."

Brax quirked a brow. "Rewind three sentences. My husband is already involved in this."

Holt was a digital assassin, Marsh's fucking protégé, who could hack all his secrets in ten minutes flat, but Marsh could try—and fail—to deter his friends. "Need to know basis."

"Marsh—"

"I'm trying to keep your family safe and in the clear. I've already told you both too much." He had no doubt the Madigans could handle anything thrown their way, but Marsh had already lost one friend to this crusade. He would avoid aiming bullets at his other ones as long as he could. "I cannot lose you too."

"Okay," Brax conceded. "But you're family too, and if you need tactical support, we'll be there."

He was lucky to call Brax family after going AWOL on him for months. Even luckier to call Lily, Holt, and the rest of the Madigans family too. They were a force to be reckoned with and more family than an only child could ever hope for. "The Madigans protect their own, I know." But he'd rather try moving this through pseudo-official channels first. He needed collars, not coffins. "You're on the call list if it comes to that."

Satisfied, Brax relented and relaxed against the rail beside him. Marsh's gaze went right back to Levi, unable to take his eyes off his new husband. He tapped his new ring against the railing, still not quite believing the whirlwind weekend that had resulted in a whirlwind marriage, even if it had all been his idea.

"You like him," Brax said.

"He's a good agent and a good father. He just needs a little help."

Brax jostled his side. "Easy on the eyes too."

Marsh chuffed. "I'm going to tell Holt."

"He's the one who said it first."

Marsh laughed out loud, drawing Levi's attention and the unguarded smile Marsh was quickly becoming addicted to. "He's also more emotionally unavailable than you or Sean ever were, which means I'm going to fall head over heels for him."

Brax scooted closer and his normally gruff voice gentled in that way that made him a good cop, a good soldier, a good husband and father. "Marsh—"

"Don't apologize."

"You give and give, Marsh, but when do you ever ask for what *you* need?"

"I'm not as selfless as you make me out to be." Just look at what he was asking of Levi. He owed Levi more than a check for risking his job and his neck.

Brax covered his hand on the railing, halting Marsh's compulsive ring tapping. "You're the most selfless man I've ever met, and I'm afraid that's gonna get you into trouble."

"What else is new?"

"Trouble you can't get out of." He rotated on his hip and squeezed Marsh's hand, demanding his full attention. "You're my best friend, Marsh. You're family. I don't want to lose you, and Lily would never forgive me if I let anything happen to her Uncle Marsh."

Marsh lifted their hands from the railing and held Brax's in both of his, letting him know how much his words meant even as he deflected. "You want to talk about trouble…"

Brax let him have the swerve, his hazel eyes fluttering closed as he sighed the sigh of a parent whose kid had him wrapped around her tiny little pinky. "You have no idea."

Oh, but he did. Two minutes with the princess and he'd been wrapped around her pinky too. "I'll be at her wedding, whenever that day comes, I promise." Just like her father had been at his.

He glanced around Brax's shoulder at his new husband, and seeing Levi's soft smile cast his way again, he was doubly grateful Brax was there. In case this turned out to be more real than either of them had bargained for.

NINE

MARSH HANDED his hat to Levi, then hauled his bags out of the cruiser. He used the weight of one to close the trunk—and came face-to-face with reality. Levi stood at the door to the right, a mat beneath his feet. Directly in front of the cars was a second door with a yellow Keep Out sign hanging from a single nail. "I can stay at the hotel another night if you want to talk to David first."

"Only delaying the inevitable," Levi said. He followed the direction of Marsh's gaze, then jutted his chin at the bike rack on the garage wall. "He's not home yet."

"How late is he usually out?" Marsh asked. By the time they'd finished at the clerk's office, had dinner with Brax and Amy, seen the former off at the airport, then swung back by the hotel to get the rest of Marsh's things, it was past eight and the summer sun was riding the horizon.

"Curfew is nine in the summer. He's at his friend's house up the street." He opened the one door and pointed at the other door. "That's his domain. Used to be a triple garage, but David wanted more privacy, and we needed a project... after..."

Something to keep their minds off the missing member of their family. Marsh got that. Hell, they'd built an entire surgical barn the summer after his stepmom, Irina's, father had passed. He rounded the front of the car and fingered the triangular sign with its smudged handprint and fake blood splatter. "Some things don't change."

"Teenage boys," Levi muttered.

"Except pot's legal now."

"He's still too young for *that*."

They were both still laughing as they entered the house through a narrow hallway, a dog's bark calling from close by. "Rest of the bedrooms are up." Levi gestured at the staircase and dropped Marsh's hat on the newel post. "I'll show you around down here first."

Following his lead, Marsh left his bags at the foot of the stairs, tossed his sport coat on top of them, and entered the great room behind Levi. His whistle echoed around the cavernous space with its high ceilings and big windows. But despite the room's size, it was cozy. Lived in. A gaming setup dominated one end of the room, a giant sectional took up the middle, and a rectangular dining table stretched under a wrought iron chandelier at the other end. "This is some setup."

"Big family that kept getting bigger, and my parents place in Pac Beach was already too small when *I* was a kid. This is where the kids today tend to congregate."

"And the adults?"

He tilted his head left, toward the back of the house, and opened a pet gate that direction. And was immediately slammed into by an excited greyhound. "Hey, Taco," he murmured to the fawn-colored dog, then to Marsh, "He's friendly."

Marsh held out a hand for the dog to sniff, and once Taco nuzzled his approval, gave him a scratch behind his velvet-soft ears.

"Oh, you might be his new best friend." Levi shut the gate behind them and draped his coat over it. "Burrito should be around here somewhere."

"Another dog?"

"Cat."

"Who gets along with this one?"

"Only when she wants to."

"Sounds about right for a cat."

Levi opened the back door with a "Let's go, boy," and Taco chose the outside over Marsh without a second thought. Marsh used the opportunity to nosy around the back half of the house. To the right was a good-sized kitchen with an island, a breakfast nook, and large picture windows. To the left was a cozy den with an oversized couch and chair and a stone fireplace. Above the fireplace, framed pictures lined a heavy wood mantel. His gaze was drawn to the photo in the middle of the collection, to Levi looking down at the fiery-haired vixen in his arms, giving her that same soft smile Marsh had caught fleeting glimpses of this afternoon. Not so fleeting back then. Levi had clearly been smitten. Who wouldn't be? Kristin's appeal—impish, playful, vibrant, alive—was undeniable, even in pictures.

Fuck.

A heavy knot of regrets and recriminations formed in his gut and plummeted to his feet, almost taking Marsh to his knees with it. What had he done? Who was he to come into this house, to interfere with this poor man's life, to even entertain the notion that the ring on Levi's finger could ever become anything as real as what he saw in that picture?

"Marsh?"

He cleared his throat and stepped away from the mantel. "I should go. I can just stay at the hotel."

"How's that gonna convince anyone?"

He cut his gaze from the photo to Levi standing in the doorway. Backlit by the setting sun, he was almost too gorgeous to look at, as fiery as his soulmate in that photo. "I can't—"

"No one's asking you to." Levi smiled, not the soft one but not a fake one either. A different one Marsh hadn't seen before, a little sad, a little resigned, a little grateful for the company. He held the door open wider. "Come see the view before the light's gone."

Marsh followed in his wake, dodging Taco who darted back inside. He stepped out the back door, onto the flag-stone patio, and almost stumbled at the view that greeted him. "Holy shit, Bishop."

"At first, I didn't want to be this deep in the burbs." He crossed to the patio's edge and rested his arms on top of the glass wall there. "I grew up in PB, close to the water and close to downtown and the heart of things, but the schools out here are better, and this view sold me."

"You don't say." A canyon stretched out below them—trails, trees, brush, and running water somewhere in the distance. It extended at least a football field across before another ridge began to climb, houses atop it too. A breeze snaked in from the west, the ocean out there somewhere behind the hills, a coyote's yips carried on the wind. "This view would sell anyone."

"Commute to the office isn't bad either," Levi added.

"This reminds me of the ranch back home."

"The canyon and coyotes?"

"No, your place. It's lived in. It's a home."

"When's the last time you had one?"

Marsh's clipped laugh scraped over shards of loneliness, coming out rougher than intended, more honest than usual. "Maybe Camp Casey. If you count officers' quarters as a home."

Levi's voice was the opposite of rough; it was too smooth for his own good. "Then pretend for a little while."

"Levi—"

"I saw you with Brax today." Surprised by the non sequitur, Marsh whipped his gaze Levi's direction, momentarily blinded by the horizon, then by the too tempting man who stepped closer. "I saw how the layer of tension you hide under your hat fell away. You were at ease with him. You were home. The way you talk about him, I'm guessing it's the same with Sean?"

"You're too perceptive."

"There's a badge in my back pocket if you want to see it." He grinned, crooked and adorable, then eased back into dangerous earnestness. "You're helping me out with my case."

"You're helping me with mine."

"Do you want to know why David was okay with this?" He didn't give Marsh time to reply, to catch up to Levi speeding around curves. "So they wouldn't repo his mother's car."

And careening off the cliff.

Without thinking, Marsh lifted a hand to Levi's cheek, the need to comfort this man who had been through too much, who was too good for the pain that had been heaped on him, impossible to resist. "Baby."

Levi leaned into the touch, and when he spoke again, his voice was lower, smooth in the *best dessert you've ever tasted* way. "You're doing more than helping me solve a case. This can't be one-sided. That's not fair." He laid a hand over Marsh's, pressing it closer, and the prickle of stubble against Marsh's palm fired all his senses, a bolt of electric heat straight to his chest. "Let me help you too. Let this be home for you for a little while."

Fucking hell.

Marsh spread his fingers, and Levi gasped. All that heat and electricity arrowed south. Not even Wile E. Coyote could stop him from drawing Levi closer, from angling his head—

The hallway door to the garage banged open.

But apparently a teenager could.

Levi flew out of his arms, faster than the Road Runner, and coupled with the guilt that swept across Levi's face, it was like someone snapped their fingers and erased the last five minutes that never should have been.

Good reminder.

"Whose Bureau cruiser is that in the garage?" David, Marsh assumed, shouted from the hallway. Confirmed when he strolled around the corner, twirling the cowboy hat around his fist, Taco dancing around him. "And since when are we into cowboy hats—" He looked up, out the door, and stopped midstep, almost tripping over Taco. His eyes grew wide, and his brows raced north, taking a face full of freckles with them. "Whoa."

"Should I call you Keanu?" Marsh replied, covering for a still out of sorts Levi standing several feet to his left.

"Who?" David asked, and Marsh groaned at the reminder of his forty-plus years on this earth.

"John Wick," he tried.

David shook his head. "Still don't get it."

Enough self-flagellation. He stepped forward, hand extended, meeting David just outside the door. "Emmitt Marshall, and that's my hat, in case the accent didn't give it away."

David handed him the hat, and as Marsh settled it back on his head, the teen's green eyes went to the band on his left ring finger. Then to the matching one on his father's. "You did it?"

"That's why I was calling all afternoon."

Hurt, plain as day, flashed across David's face, and Levi stepped forward, only to have his path cut off by the dog. By the time he shooed Taco out of the way, David had straightened and brought up his resting teen face. The expressive equivalent of *whatever*. "It's not real anyway." Except his added, "Where's he sleeping?" gave away more than he realized.

"The guest room," Levi answered.

"Your dad tells me you play chess," Marsh said. "Care to get to know me over the board?"

"You play?" An interested crack in the façade.

"A little."

"Maybe in the morning. I'm beat."

He turned to leave, but Levi called him back, asking pointedly, "Where are you on the summer reading list?"

The answering whine was epic. "It hasn't even been a month since I got done with school." Marsh muffled his laugh.

"You can't spend all day in front of the computer."

He rolled his eyes, so similar to how Levi rolled his at times that Marsh did laugh then, and the tension that had been hanging over them since the near kiss dissipated completely, Levi chuckling too as he stepped next to Marsh. "Two books by the end of the month," he told David. "And introduce yourself properly."

"David Bishop. Don't hurt my dad."

"Wouldn't dream of it."

"And be ready to get beat tomorrow morning."

An in; Marsh would take it. "Looking forward to it."

His muttered "Sucker" as he turned the corner to his room was bested by Levi's "You're gonna kick his ass, aren't you?"

He needed to win the kid over but not at the expense of his chess game. "Oh yeah."

TEN

TEN DAYS.

Ten days Marsh had been living with them, and every morning that Levi returned from his morning run to the smell of freshly brewed coffee wafting out of the kitchen made him grab the door to stay upright. Sure, he cranked up the espresso machine for family gatherings, but that had been the extent of its use the past two years. Not every morning, not multiple times a day, not like Kristin used to wear it out. It was both a blessing and curse to relive the memories of their family routine that used to be. Impossible not to compare it to the one they were settling into now. One he hadn't asked Marsh to stop. Hadn't asked him to go out and pick up coffee from someplace else. He'd meant what he'd said about wanting Marsh to feel at home, and to Levi, the past ten days were the first time in two years his house had felt like a home. Life was returning to normal— the smell of morning coffee, no teen outbursts, no collection calls, a third person knocking around the house with him, David, and the pets.

Legs steadier, Levi continued up the stairs but paused before turning to his room, pivoting instead to the rest of the upstairs. The office door was locked as he and Marsh had agreed to keep it. The guest bathroom was spotless, the bedroom beside it the same. Levi recognized the military-trained neatness from his own childhood—glass shower walls squeegeed down, toiletry kit tucked away, bed perfectly made, everything where it belonged. Except the tabby furball curled on the middle bed pillow. "I see how it is," Levi muttered. Burrito lifted her head, blinked her big yellow eyes, a barely there acknowledgment, then snuggled back down with a go-away tail flick. If he had to guess, that was the pillow Marsh had slept on.

He left the cat to her new favorite spot, returned to his room to shower and dress, then followed the sound of voices to the kitchen. Marsh and David were seated on either side of the breakfast table, Marsh's chess board between them. Levi had noticed the travel set at the hotel, but over the past ten days, he'd seen more of the wooden box that held chess pieces and, when unlatched and unfolded, flattened out to a board. He'd come to appreciate the hand-carved details of the board and pieces and the chips and scrapes that indicated a treasure well loved, well traveled, and well used.

"I see what you did there," David said, so focused on the board Levi wondered if he'd noticed his entrance. "You're setting up a king hunt."

"A what?" Levi asked.

"I'm trying to flush out his king," Marsh said. "I want to draw him to my side of the board where I have more protection, power, and maneuverability." Then he said to David, "Question is, how are you going to counter?"

Chin in hand, David contemplated while Taco skirted between his legs under the table, darting for Levi and staring up at him with pleading eyes. "Did anyone feed the dog?"

Marsh lifted two fingers but didn't look away from the board. "Twice. Don't let him fool you too."

"Critical position, Dad," David said, his dismissive wave so similar to Burrito's tail flick that Levi chuckled. Sure, it stung a little, but the positive changes in David over the past ten days were as good as any balm.

He bent and scratched behind Taco's ears. "Sorry, buddy. They ratted you out." He booped his pink nose. "I'll let you lick the bowls when we're done." Good enough for Taco, the big beast sprawling in a sunny spot on the floor while Levi got the oatmeal going in the pressure cooker. He set the toppings, bowls, and spoons on the island, then took his cup of tea outside to the patio, enjoying the morning sun as birds zoomed to and from the feeders.

"Goddammit," David cursed.

"Language," Levi corrected through the open windows.

"Sorry," David replied, sounding like he meant it for a change. Levi smiled. Smiled wider at the tone of his "Show me how you did it?" to Marsh. A question, not a brusque teenage demand, and as Marsh explained the maneuver, as David asked follow-up questions with an excitement in his voice that had been missing for so long, more of that peaceful normalcy swept over Levi.

"He's good," Marsh said a few minutes later as he joined Levi at the patio table with two bowls of steaming oatmeal. He slid the bowl with coconut shavings and dried cranberries on top in front of Levi. "There a chess club at school?"

"At the high school he starts at next year."

"I have some computer programs and training sims I can share with him in the meantime."

"That would be great, thank you. He hasn't been this excited about anything, not even his video games, in a while."

"It's nice to have someone to play against over the board, in person. I'm never sure when Brax makes a bone-headed move if it's him being an idiot or if it's Lily punching buttons." He dug into his bowl of oatmeal, doctored with butter, brown sugar, and cinnamon, and hummed with delight. Levi wondered what that hum, just on the decent side of a growl, might sound like in a less decent context. Not too hard to imagine with Marsh sitting there in the morning sun, his bronze skin aglow and his dark grabbable hair ruffled by the breeze, in his usual morning attire of sweats, a T-shirt, and black-rimmed glasses. Levi dropped his gaze to his oatmeal before his dick got any more interested.

"You know," Marsh said, "you're not a half-bad cook, and you pay attention." He gestured with his topping-laden spoon.

"I was the oopsie baby, seven years after Nicole, nine after Bella, ten after Amy. By the time I came along, there was a lot Mom and Dad had to pay for with my sisters' activities and school. Mom worked two jobs, and Dad was either working on base or deployed, so as soon as I was tall enough to reach the cooktop, I started cooking. As for noticing you have a sweet tooth that rivals Kwan's, I'll remind you about that badge in my pocket."

Marsh chuffed, his cheeks rosy, and Levi didn't think it was only the sun that had caused his blush, or Levi's, both of them recalling the quiet closeness of that night after the wedding when they'd almost—

Levi cut off the memory, even if his mind and body ached for that sort of intimacy again. They'd barely touched since then, had kept a careful distance between them as if they both knew that way led to temptation.

Led to a less than professional arrangement.

"Speaking of our employer," Marsh said, "I'm coming in today."

"To the office?" He'd popped in one other day the previous week, but only long enough to turn in the disclosures and other necessary forms. Otherwise, he'd been working from the office upstairs.

"Kwan will have cooled off by now, and we need to sell this. Us together and me checking out the office for a possible transfer."

Levi dropped his spoon into the bowl, pushed it aside, and propped his elbows on the table. He scrubbed his hands over his face, mourning the loss of the peaceful mood.

Marsh ran a hand up and down his spine. "You can do this."

His voice was as warm as his touch, as warm as the morning sun bathing them both, and Levi wanted to drown in it, wanted to use it as a shield against the day ahead. He lowered his hands, forearms resting on the table. "I don't like lying to her or to Matt and my team."

"You're not technically lying." Marsh flitted his ring hand in the air, sunlight catching the metal and drawing Levi's gaze. "And I have other matters I need to check up on. I'd rather do that with Bureau resources than my own." He stood, gathered the bowls, and hip-checked Levi's shoulder before heading toward the open back door. "Time to cowboy up, Agent Bishop."

Levi smiled despite the challenges of the day ahead. Smiled wider as he listened to Marsh inside, checking in with David once more, then letting Taco lick their bowls as Levi had promised. Marsh paid attention too, was smarter than Levi had initially given him credit for. Maybe he would be right about the office too. He twirled his ring around his finger. Things had improved at home with Marsh. He hoped Marsh was right and the same would hold true at the office.

♟♞♝♚♛♝♞♟

OR NOT. They were barely off the elevator, Levi flashing his key card to enter, Marsh his visitor's pass, when the receptionist chirped that the ASAC wanted to see Marsh in her office ASAP.

"Yes, ma'am," Marsh said, his charming grin in place. The smile wasn't quite so bright once inside Levi's office, but he didn't seem ruffled by the summons. "Standard operating procedure," he said with more steadiness than Levi felt. "It's like this in any office I visit. Meet with the higher-ups, brief them on our international positions. There's a benefit to knowing the larger picture."

"And we didn't get that far last time," Levi reasoned. Put together another picture too. "Last week when we came in, Kwan wasn't here. Was that on purpose?"

Marsh shrugged.

"Thought so." Before he could give Marsh any more of his thoughts, Matt appeared in the doorway.

"Hey, Marsh," he greeted. "Thanks again for that information on the jewel thieves. Helped connect some dots."

"Was hoping it might."

He turned his attention to Levi and gestured with the folder in his hand. "I've got a lead on that white-collar case we're working."

"And I better go see Kwan." Marsh squeezed his biceps and dropped a quick kiss on his cheek that didn't burn any less for its brevity. "I'll let you know which broom closet she sticks me in."

"Good luck." Levi hoped his voice didn't sound as wobbly as his knees felt.

"I still can't wrap my head around it," Matt said, giving voice to Levi's thoughts. "Or figure out how you kept a lid on it—and him."

"We had to be careful." Levi twirled his wedding band around his finger. "And he was an ocean away."

"Well, at least you didn't have to do it for long."

"It's been a whirlwind." Not a lie and not what they needed to focus on. He grasped instead at the concrete case in front of him. "Show me what you've got on the white-collar matter."

Celome Logistics had offices in multiple states, making the suspected embezzlement raised by one of its board members to Celome's company counsel a federal investigation. Forensic accounting was underway and, judging by the documents Matt had spread out over his desk, was producing interesting results.

"What Marsh said the other day about our trafficking case—about the overpayments—got me thinking. What if that's what's going on at Celome? This"—he pushed a payment receipt in front of Levi—"is too much money for the items listed on this"—he pushed forward a purchase order—"PO. I called the vendor." He set his tablet on top of the papers, the calculator open, a much lower number displayed. "This is what it was supposed to cost."

"Are there other POs like this one?"

"A dozen others so far." He slid several other sheets of paper across the desk toward Levi. "See anything in common?"

It didn't take Levi long to detect the matching signature on each of them. "They're all signed by Tiffany Burton. She got a record?"

Matt shook his head. "Clean."

"Off the record?"

"Single mom struggling to make ends meet."

A pang of sympathy shot through Levi. He could commiserate with Ms. Burton. He'd also taken drastic measures to make some of those ends meet—he twirled the ring around his finger again—but his actions weren't technically illegal. Maybe Ms. Burton's weren't either, but the POs in front of him were awfully damning. "Let's go chat with Ms. Burton."

ELEVEN

LEVI WAITED in what appeared to be Celome Logistics' primary conference room, watching out the window as two fighter jets rocketed into the sky. Celome was among the cluster of logistics companies in the industrial area along the north side of Miramar Road. On the south side of the road was Marine Corp Air Station Miramar.

"You know," Matt said from the table behind him, "I thought that was *so* cool the first few months I was here. Now, the *Top Gun* of it all has worn off."

Levi chuckled, surprised at the normally chipper agent's gripe. Would the racket eventually become white noise to Matt as it was to Levi, or would it chase him away as it had done so many of Levi's friends, classmates, and colleagues? Not everyone could tolerate the frequent roar of jet engines, the whir and thump of choppers, even the sonic booms that happened more often than was legal. With three major military bases in San Diego County, there was no escaping it. It was sometimes problematic for veterans and others who'd escaped conflict zones, but Marsh, Levi realized, hadn't so much as blinked, flinched, or even looked up when jets and choppers regularly flew over the house and office. Fifteen years on an active military base in Afghanistan would probably white noise the hell out of San Diego's military racket. He was the rare person who could move here and skip the usual adjustment period.

Not that he had moved here. Permanently.

Levi shook off the thought and the cascade of images of a well-settled Marsh, turning his back to the window and impossibilities. He slid into the chair next to Matt near one end of the table, then stood the next second as the receptionist, Amanda Hudson her badge read, led another woman into the room. "Gentlemen," Amanda said, "This is Tiffany Burton." Amanda tossed them a flirtatious smile, practically ignoring Ms. Burton beside her. "You need anything else?"

"We're good," Matt said with a wink that made Amanda's freshly painted lips curve more. She twirled a dark ringlet around her finger, pouting when Matt dismissed her, albeit kindly. "Thank you, Amanda."

She backed out the door, leaving Ms. Burton standing just inside the room, hands clasped in front of her. She was a white woman, late thirties, with blond hair and brown eyes. Her back was straight, her head held high, but her gaze bounced between him and Matt and the knuckles on her hand clutching the other were white, betraying her nerves. "What's this about?"

"Ms. Burton," Levi said, "please have a seat." He gestured to the chair at the head of the table, a favorite tactic of his when questioning someone. It gave the other person a sense of security that often translated to more answers and better cooperation. They waited for her to sit, then Levi, after withdrawing his badge, lowered himself next to Matt again. "I'm Special Agent Levi Bishop." He flashed his badge and Matt did the same. "And this is Special Agent Matthew Kim. We're with the FBI."

"The FBI?" Her voice rose. "What does the FBI want with me?" A moment later, a mental light bulb went off for Ms. Burton and wrinkles crinkled her forehead. "Wait, does this have something to do with the records request earlier this month?"

"We're investigating some unusual financial activity here at Celome." On the way over, he and Matt had discussed how much to disclose to Ms. Burton. It was always a risk, but the reaction of the person they were questioning was often more than worth it.

"Unusual financial activity?"

Case in point, Ms. Burton's surprise appeared genuine. That or she was a fantastic actress. Yet not good enough to cover her nervous ticks earlier? And not good enough to hide the weariness that belied how well put together she looked on first glance? The roots of her blond hair were gray—overdue for an appointment. There was a stain on the collar of her dress shirt—probably from where she'd burped her toddler that morning. Her makeup was applied unevenly—done in a hurry, probably in the car on her way to the office. Her shoulders slumped before she remembered to adjust her posture again.

"Ms. Burton," Levi said, "can you tell us what you do here at Celome Logistics?"

"My job?"

Levi nodded.

"What does my job have to do with unusual financial activity?" she asked. When Levi didn't reply, she glanced at

Matt, who likewise didn't answer. They'd reached the limit on the information they'd agreed to give her to start.

"Fine." She adjusted in her chair, sitting in it more fully and rolling the chair closer to the table. Levi was familiar with that trick too, using the chair to keep his back straight, to prop him up when he barely had the energy to do it himself. Ms. Burton was exhausted. "I'm the head of purchasing here at Celome," she said.

"For this location?" Matt asked, adopting an icier tone.

"Nationwide."

"And what does being the head of purchasing involve?"

She cocked her head and raised a brow, the *are you idiots* glare a welcome break in the tension.

Both he and Matt laughed, and Levi let that bleed into a more casual tone, a lighter mood that would hopefully yield more answers. "What does it involve here at Celome, Ms. Burton? In our experience, it varies company to company."

"Fair enough, and please, call me Tiffany." Relaxing, she leaned forward and folded her arms on the table, fingers no longer in a death grip. "I have the relationship with our vendors, so I work with my team to do all the sourcing and ordering. We've found a single point of contact works best for procurement and for getting supply chain info to the internal folks who need to know. They then communicate with our customers."

"How many people are on your team?" Matt asked.

"Me, two direct reports, and an assistant. It was just me and Von, our assistant, until we stood up sites in Austin and Atlanta last year. We needed more help with forecasting, analysis, and record keeping."

"But all purchase orders still come through you?"

"That's correct."

"You review each one?"

She nodded. "The person in charge of budgeting for each of the company's cost centers submits their POs through an online portal. Von checks over each one and the supporting documents submitted with it. He runs down any missing info, checks with Crystal and DJ, those are the other two people on our team, to make sure the request is in line with our forecasting and analysis, then submits the PO to me."

Matt pulled a folder from where he'd tucked it beside him in the chair. "Do these look familiar to you?" He opened the folder and pushed three of the suspect POs in front of Tiffany.

She flipped through the papers. "They're purchase orders on our standard form."

"And you signed each one?"

"That's right."

"Do they look to be in order?"

She didn't answer right away, the couple seconds of hesitation letting on that she likely followed where Matt was going. "They look to be," she hedged. "But I review at least fifty of these a da—" She lurched forward, yanking one of the POs closer. "This isn't right."

"What's not right?" Levi said.

"This piece of equipment here." She pointed at one of the line items with a chipped nail. "This wasn't the price I approved."

"But you just said you review at least fifty of these a day. You would remember the price on this one line item?"

"The damn thing is a beast, and it cost six hundred sixty-six dollars."

"I can see how that would be hard to forget."

"Exactly." Standing, she stepped around the table to the door and stuck her head out. "Amanda," she called to the receptionist. There was a phone in the middle of the table, but if it was anything like the Bureau's conference room phones, the door was an easier option. "Can you please ask Von to bring me my laptop?"

Amanda hopped up from her desk, and Tiffany returned to her seat, taking a closer look at the other purchase orders. "These are wrong too." She pointed at two line items on the second PO. "I negotiated a price reduction for both of these." Then gestured at the third. "And this one's for a recurring monthly order. The price never changes." Her face blanched and her breath hitched, the pieces coming together in her head. "They're all higher." Her wide-eyed gaze shot up. "I didn't have anything to do with this."

"But your signature is on all of them," Levi said.

"Maybe you missed these?" Matt jutted his chin at the stack of POs. "Things are hectic at home."

Her eyes narrowed. "How do you know that?" Same as before, he and Matt gave her nothing more. Same as before, she filled the void. "I can prove those aren't the POs I approved. I have backups. Where is Amanda?" She stood and turned for the door again, only to halt as a slim Black man appeared in the doorway. Whatever he saw caused him to step closer, his free hand immediately going to Tiffany's forearm. "Is everything okay?"

Her smile was tight and not at all convincing. "Just needed my laptop to help clear something up."

Von handed her the computer. "Amanda left for an early lunch. I'll wait at the reception desk in case you need me."

Me, not *anything*. Together with his soft concerned voice and lingering gaze, Levi would bet Von and Tiffany were involved or wanted to be if not for whatever had made a mess of Tiffany's life. Embezzlement, maybe? After Von left, Tiffany sank back into her chair and opened her laptop. "Should I have a lawyer here? Or the company lawyer?"

"If you've got the backups," Matt said, "shouldn't be an issue."

Her fingers moved across the keyboard at a fast clip. Not Marsh fast but *types a lot for a living* fast. "I save a copy of each PO and supporting doc in an encrypted file on a private server."

"That's some foresight." Probably also against company policy.

"My late husband was cyber security at Miramar."

So that's why she was resisting Von's overtures. Levi felt another pang of shared sympathy for Ms. Burton. "I'm sorry for your loss."

"You have no idea." She finished typing and glanced up, and contrary to Von's reaction earlier, whatever she saw on Levi's face smoothed over her nerves. "Or maybe you do." She nodded, acknowledgment and commiseration of their shared, unfortunate circumstances. "These are the POs I signed," she said, voice less defensive, more cooperative.

"Why didn't you produce these in the records request?" Levi asked, keeping his tone conversational, not accusatory. They were making headway he did not want to jeopardize.

"I had no reason to think they were different."

"We need to find out how they were changed," Matt said.

"I can alert our IT team."

Matt shook his head. "We don't know where it was changed. It could be someone on your IT team."

"I can ask one of my late husband's colleagues. Plenty of them are still at Miramar or in the private sector around here."

Levi spun the band on his left ring finger, thinking of another cyber military vet. "I might have someone who could help."

"Ya think?" Matt jutted a thumb at him. "His new husband is a cyber agent. Also ex-military."

Tiffany grinned, a good five years falling off her exhausted exterior. "Good for you," she said with a pat to his hand. "Gives all of us some hope." She grabbed a branded scratch pad and pen from the supply caddy by the phone. "This is the cloud-based site our PO portal runs on," she said as she scribbled. "And the username and password if your husband needs them." She ripped off the top sheet and handed it to Levi.

"I'll just be a minute." He stood and walked to the other end of the conference room, dialing Marsh.

"Hey," Marsh answered on the second ring. "How's it going there?"

Levi smirked at the yawn Marsh tried and failed to cover with his words. "Could use your hacker help on something unless you need more bean water first."

"Just for that, you can pick up a venti honey vanilla latte for me on your way back to the office."

Levi's smirk became a smile. "With whip?"

"Of course with whip. What kind of a fool question is that?"

"Figured as much." A chuckle escaped before Levi got down to business. "I've got some altered purchase orders here. Employee stored backups of the originals. They don't match the ones that went through the cloud-based PO portal for payment."

"Smart. Address and login?"

He rattled them off to Marsh, and a few seconds later, he was in. "Give me a second to orient myself and look at the docs and code," Marsh said. "You said POs?"

"That's right."

"Okay, got 'em. Which ones?"

Levi recited the PO numbers from memory.

Keystrokes resumed, a rising crescendo, Marsh on the hunt. "Altered is right," he said after another minute. "I've got overwrites on all three, each on the day of payment."

"And the original amounts?"

Marsh read off the amounts, which were a match to Tiffany's backups.

"Can you tell who changed them?" Levi asked.

"Same user." Marsh provided the three-letter, four-digit username, and Levi asked Tiffany if she recognized the user.

"That's Johnny Norris," she answered. "He works in accounting. Two floors up." Her forehead creased, and she whipped around in her chair, glancing the direction of the reception desk. "He's also Amanda's boyfriend."

Amanda, the receptionist who still hadn't returned, Von sitting alone at the lobby desk.

Matt bolted out of his seat and was at the door by the time Levi rounded the other end of the table. "Where are the stairs?"

"Through the lobby and to the right. Second door on the right." Tiffany yanked the access badge off her jacket lapel and tossed it across the table to Levi. "You'll need this."

"Thank you."

He and Matt sprinted across the lobby, Von's "What's going on?" an echo behind them as Levi swiped Tiffany's badge and led Matt through the lobby doors. They hung a right, used the access badge again to bang through the second door, then charged up the stairs, eating the steps two at a time. Levi paused outside the door two floors up, badge hovering short of the keypad. "Containment," he told Matt. "No collateral. We go in quiet. Ask the first person we see where Johnny is."

"You got it," Matt said, adjusting his jacket.

Levi flashed the key card over the pad, and Matt opened the door, coming face-to-face with a woman stepping out of a supply closet across the hallway, her arms full of folders and legal pads. Her gaze flitted over them, and she clutched her supplies closer to her chest, no doubt alarmed at seeing strangers on her floor. But then her gaze dropped to their visitor stickers and she eased her grip a measure. "Can I help you?"

"We're looking for Johnny Norris," Matt said. "Von said we could find him on this floor."

"Usually, yes, but he left for lunch with his girlfriend about ten minutes ago." Nerves gone, she coyly shrugged a single shoulder. "Maybe I can show you around?"

"Thanks for the offer," Matt said, more charming than Levi would have been able to manage. "We'll try to catch up to Johnny downstairs." Matt waited until she turned the corner to utter the truth. "They're long gone by now."

Levi's assessment as he slumped against the wall was more succinct. "Fuck."

TWELVE

MARSH DIDN'T HAVE to look up from Levi's dual monitors to know who stood in the office doorway, pointedly clearing his throat. "Community property," Marsh said.

"Or someone didn't play nice with the other nerds," his husband replied. "I assume that's where Kwan put you."

"You assume correctly." He finished organizing his search results and lifted his fingers off the keyboard, giving them a stretch. "They're actually pretty cool, but I needed access to your case file." He slumped back in Levi's perfectly broken-in office chair. "And your chair is far superior."

"How'd you get into my— You know what, never mind."

"Smart man." Marsh smirked and tilted his head toward the screens. "You won't care when I show you what I've found going on at Celome."

Levi tossed his coat on the back of the visitor chair and circled the desk, leaning a hip against the edge near Marsh.

Marsh scooted closer and rubbed Levi's outer arm. "Sorry the bad guys got away." Levi had called from the car to update him on Amanda and Johnny's getaway. That's when Marsh had decided to dig more, to help lessen the blow if he could.

"Happens more often than the TV shows let on."

"Doesn't it, though?"

Levi's hand atop his was warm and so casually intimate that more moments like it—fantasies—began to unspool in Marsh's head. Fingers brushing over morning coffee and tea. A lingering hand on his cowboy hat. Their hands tangling on the console between car seats.

Levi removed his hand and curled it around the lip of the desk. "What've you got?" he asked.

Back to reality, then. Marsh clicked to bring forward one of the documents on-screen. "First, I called the vendors to confirm how much they were paid. Exactly the amounts on Tiffany's original purchase orders. But these are the amounts that went out."

Levi leaned closer, over his shoulder. "Those match the amounts on the altered purchase orders."

"They do. And guess who's responsible for pushing the button to send out the payments?"

"Johnny Norris?"

"No."

Levi's head jerked back like a funky chicken. "No?"

Marsh had to laugh. Would've kept laughing if not for Levi kicking his shin. "Sorry, couldn't help it." He reined in the hilarity, then pulled forward a picture. "Frederick Beach."

"Who the hell is Frederick Beach?"

Marsh brought forward an account register. "Between

Celome and the supplier is an ACH processor. That's where Frederick works, and that's where the extra money is split off. The correct amount goes to the vendor, the extra goes into this account, which looks like a holding account for Celome."

"But it's not."

"It's not. In fact, not a single employee at Celome has access to it. Only Frederick Beach."

Levi touched the screen, and this time Marsh did bat his hand away.

"It's my screen!" Levi scoffed, then tapped it again, the irritating asshole. "The extra amount is the difference in the POs. What happens to the money from there?"

"It's used to purchase bitcoin, a.k.a. Money Laundering 101, but here's the interesting part..." He pulled up two bitcoin account records. "Ten percent of those bitcoin purchases are then transferred to a second bitcoin account."

"One for Frederick, one for Johnny?"

Marsh nodded. "That's what I'm thinking. We need a warrant to get to the bitcoin account holders."

"You can't hack that info?"

While Levi had been smart enough not to ask the access question earlier, he was less so now. Marsh picked up the slack, understanding the temptation better than anyone. "I can try, but—"

Levi crossed his arms and puffed out his chest, looking cocky and confident, which did all sorts of twisty things to Marsh's insides. "What kind of cowboy are you?"

"The kind whose ass is already too close to the fire."

"It's a nice ass. Wouldn't want it burned."

The knots untangled, all those feelings arrowing straight to Marsh's dick. It must have shown on his face, or behind the fly of his jeans, because Levi smirked deeper, a goddamn dimple appearing in one cheek. Un-fucking-fair.

"Objective observation," Levi added, sounding rather subjective.

"I'm your husband. Screw objective."

His smirk eased into a smile. "Sounds like I need to get started on a warrant request, but someone's in my chair."

Marsh stood, bringing them too close for professional, but fuck it. Levi had trotted out that dimple, and all was lost. "When you're done, the last file I opened for you are Johnny's, Frederick's, and Amanda's addresses." He rubbed Levi's arm, same as he had before. "You know, if we wanted to go ahead and question them."

Levi covered Marsh's hand, holding it right where Marsh wanted to be. Close. "We? You don't have other casework?"

"Triad theft of IP. Calls with Hong Kong later today."

Levi flicked his gaze at the screens. "And I'm guessing this is more fun than chasing counterfeit electronics."

Marsh winked. "Like I said, smart man."

♟♙♟♙♙♙♟♙♙

MARSH UNFOLDED from the passenger seat of the RX and met Levi and Matt at the front of the vehicle. "Fingers crossed we have better luck with this one."

They'd gone to Frederick's house first on the off chance they reached him before news that someone had caught on to his scheme did. According to his employer, Frederick worked from home, but by the time they got there, Frederick's place was locked up tight, no car in the driveway and no life inside. A quick on-site hack of his home monitoring system, which was disappointingly easy to access for a guy who dealt in bitcoin, confirmed Frederick had left shortly after Johnny and Amanda had left Celome.

Marsh bet they were all together somewhere, sorting out a plan. If it had just been Johnny, or only Johnny or Amanda, a quick getaway might have been possible. But the more people involved in a conspiracy, the harder it was to cover up or disappear. Which gave Marsh, Levi, and Matt the upper hand. Chances were they'd find the trio of thieves before said thieves got their shit together.

Would that be at Johnny's place in a neighborhood Levi had called Del Cerro? From what Marsh could tell, they were halfway up a giant hill, the freeways crisscrossing below and larger houses looming above. But the street they walked along was relatively flat and the fronts of the lots the same. The houses looked to be from the fifties, sixties, and seventies, slightly larger than what Marsh was used to seeing in the Bay Area, more than a few recently renovated and sold judging by their fresh coats of paint and unseasonably green grass.

Johnny's house still had the Sold sign in the front yard. He'd closed on the place just last week. A million-dollar home purchased by a guy who legally cleared a hundred thousand a year. According to Johnny's tax returns, he didn't have any other sources of income. As they neared the property, Levi raised a fist, signaling Marsh and Matt to halt. Raised voices drifted from inside the house. At Levi's signal, they ducked behind the fence that framed the lot and provided privacy from the neighbors.

"Cameras?" Levi whispered. "Home security?"

Matt peeked around the edge of the fence. "I don't see any cameras."

"Listing said the house came with a security system," Marsh said. "Might not be activated yet." He tapped his phone, opening the list of nearby wireless networks. "Nothing coming from Johnny's place."

"Exit routes?" Levi asked.

"Nowhere they can go in the back," Marsh said. "It's a cliff. The lot drops off." The topography map showed a steep slope to an aqueduct below, the freeways on the other side.

"Front of the house?" Levi asked Matt.

"Front door, garage door, probably a side door off the garage."

Levi rose on his toes, peeking over the top of the fence. "No door on this side."

"I'll go to the front door," Marsh suggested. "I wasn't at Celome. They don't know me, and let's be honest, do I look like a fed?"

Matt gave his dark jeans, button-up with no coat or tie, and black Stetson a once-over. "He's got a point."

Levi rolled his eyes with a muttered, "Don't encourage him," but then grudgingly agreed. Levi and Matt stepped out from behind the fence first and strolled along the sidewalk in what appeared to be quiet conversation. Once they reached the far property line, they plastered themselves to the fence and skirted down the inside length of it, taking up position behind the garage corner. Marsh counted to ten before reemerging onto the sidewalk but only for the few steps it took to reach the front walkway. He turned down it, moving determinedly to the front door and ringing the doorbell.

Inside, the voices quieted. No footsteps approached.

Marsh rang the doorbell again and leaned to the side, looking through the front window and catching sight of Johnny standing on one side of a kitchen island. Midthirties, white, below average weight, above average height, shaggy dark hair. He glanced toward the door, and Marsh waved. "Try ignoring me now, dumbass," he mumbled behind a smile.

Johnny's attention whipped back to someone across the island from him out of Marsh's sight. Amanda or Frederick? Marsh thought he'd heard a woman's voice inside, but he couldn't be sure. Marsh raised his fist to knock, to make sure Johnny knew he'd seen him and wasn't going away, but lowered it when footsteps grew louder, moving toward the door.

Johnny opened it far enough to poke his head out. "Closest rodeo's out in Lakeside."

Marsh dialed the accent up, playing into the awwshucks of it all and into Johnny's assumptions about it, making himself seem like less of a threat. "I'm looking for Johnny Norris. Is that you? My realtor said she knows your realtor and that you're selling."

"You're selling?" Amanda appeared at the entrance to the kitchen behind him. Still dressed in work clothes, she stood with her hands on her suited hips, angry red streaks coloring her cheekbones. "You just bought the place."

Startled, Johnny opened the door wider, and Marsh took advantage. Foot wedged against the bottom, hand splayed in the middle, he shoved the door out of Johnny's grip, wide enough to step through. "Amanda Hudson?" Marsh said.

Johnny stepped between them. "How do you know her name?"

Marsh withdrew his badge. "Special Agent Emmitt Marshall."

Three things happened at once: a vehicle cranked to the left, the direction of the garage; Amanda grabbed a nearby bottle, broke it against the kitchen island, and hurled it, jagged edge out, Marsh's direction before bolting across the living room toward the garage; and Johnny spun to run after her. Marsh dodged the bottle and lurched forward, grabbing Johnny by the back of his T-shirt. Johnny raised his arms, trying to use the hold to slip out of the shirt, but Marsh had at least fifty pounds on him. Putting the shirt to the use he wanted, Marsh caged Johnny's arms and yanked them behind his back. Johnny screamed in pain, and Marsh kicked at the back of his knees, sending him tumbling to the ground, knees crunching glass. Front flat on the fake hardwood floor, Johnny finally stilled with his arms pinned behind him and Marsh's knee in his back.

The vehicle in the garage revved and the garage door engaged, cranking as it began to lift. "Get clear!" Marsh shouted out the open door behind him.

"FBI! Stop!" Levi shouted, echoed by Matt's, "Put the car in park!"

Frederick, if Marsh had to guess, ignored their warnings. He gunned the vehicle's engine and tires squealed. Heart in his throat, Marsh yanked his cuffs out of his back pocket, snapped one end around Johnny's wrist, the other around the horizontal base bar of the heavy entry table, then scrambled up and out the door just in time to see Levi dive out of a speeding SUV's path.

From the driveway's other side, Matt appeared with an

old fence plank in hand. He slung it, rusty nails up, into the car's path, and its tires popped. The vehicle careened out of control, fishtailing across the driveway, barely giving Marsh time to yank Levi out of the way, rolling them so Marsh's back was to the debris that blasted their direction when the SUV finally hit the retaining wall surrounding the driveway.

The next instant, before Marsh could assess if there were any injuries, before he could tighten his arms around Levi and send up a prayer of thanks, Levi pushed them the rest of the way over and bounded up, weapon drawn and charging toward the SUV. "FBI! Freeze!" he shouted at Amanda through the passenger window.

Matt was on the other side of the vehicle, shouting the same at Frederick. The SUV gave a final sad whine and emitted a pitiful puff of smoke. Game over. Frederick and Amanda raised their hands, surrendering, and as Marsh watched Levi direct them out of the car and onto the ground, efficiently getting them and the scene secure, Marsh surrendered a little more of his heart to the man who continued to impress him.

THIRTEEN

LEVI CLOSED the interrogation room door, leaving Johnny to stew alone inside, and found Matt leaning against the hallway wall outside. Head hung, shoulders slumped, he looked as exhausted and frustrated as Levi felt after the past hour of Johnny's stonewalling. "I got nothing," Levi said, resting next to him. "You get anything out of Amanda?"

"Nada." Matt lifted his head. "Claims she knows nothing about the changed purchase orders or about bitcoin."

"Same from Johnny."

"Well, that's a fucking lie," Marsh called from the observation room across the hall.

Levi pushed off the wall and bit back a wince, the day's earlier tumble outside Johnny's house catching up to him. His shoulder ached, his knee twinged with every step, and his hip felt like it was sixty, not thirty-eight. Maybe he'd take a bath when he got home. Maybe Marsh would— He shoved the thought aside, same as he had the lingering sensation of Marsh's solid front against his back and his big arms around him. The moment was short lived, ninety-five percent of his brain at the time occupied with avoiding the swerving SUV, but the other five percent had relished the close contact and longed for more. Which couldn't be his focus now, shouldn't be his focus at all.

Professional, he chided himself and gave his head a hard shake before stepping into the observation room where Marsh worked on the other side of the glass from Frederick. "Warrant came through?" Levi asked.

"Already got the bitcoin account info." Marsh gestured at his laptop screen where two account ledgers were open. "Left one belongs to Frederick, the right one to Johnny."

"What about Amanda?" Matt said, entering behind him.

"Doesn't have one, and neither Frederick's nor Johnny's bitcoin accounts are linked to any account of hers I can find. I can't figure out how she's tied to this other than as Johnny's girlfriend."

"Anything from the search you started earlier?" Levi asked.

"Nothing," Marsh replied. "There's little to connect her to Johnny besides Celome and their relationship, even less to connect her to Frederick. I didn't find any deposits from either of them into any of her accounts."

"Cash?" Matt suggested.

"Could be. Frederick, though"—he nodded at the man on the other side of the glass—"is the one who pulls the trigger *and* the one with the more interesting account history."

"How so?" Levi asked.

Marsh maximized the window that displayed Frederick's account ledger. "Anything look familiar?"

Leaning over Marsh's shoulder, Levi ignored the distracting lure of leather and tea tree oil and skimmed the list of transactions, halting at line five. "That's the same bank our traffickers use."

Marsh opened a spreadsheet displaying multiple groups of transactions. "One of these might even be your traffickers."

"Fuck." Matt reached over Marsh's opposite shoulder and pointed to one of the groups. "It's that one. The dates line up."

"Freddy Boy's got quite the side hustle, funneling money through bitcoin accounts and skimming some for himself."

"And he used the same technique to embezzle from Celome?" Levi said. "For a scheme Johnny cooked up?"

"Why?" Matt said, echoing the final question in Levi's mind. "He's making plenty laundering for criminals."

"Some idiots are danger junkies," Marsh said. "Or really fucking greedy."

Levi didn't buy it. "Something else is going on, and we need to know what." He glanced again at the group of suspect transactions. "Same account we previously tied to the traffickers?"

Marsh nodded. "Orchard Investments, LLC."

Levi flicked his gaze to Frederick, then to Matt. "Got enough to take a run at this guy?"

"I should hope so." Matt retrieved three earpieces out of the desk drawer, tucked one into his ear, then handed one to Levi and the other to Marsh. "Listen in, keep hacking, feed us anything your searches turn up."

"Roger that."

Matt opened the interrogation room door, and Levi

moved to follow, only to be drawn back, one of Marsh's strong arms Levi hadn't been thinking about snaking around his waist and pulling him closer. Levi's insides swooped, and his heart climbed into his throat. With all Marsh's warm strength around him, his head against Levi's chest, there was nothing Levi could do but lift a hand and card it through his thick dark waves, the strands of silver dancing under the overheads. Levi inhaled, drowning in the scents of his fantasies. "What's this for?" he whispered hoarsely.

"Because I didn't get to do it when you dodged that car."

Oh.

Words deserted Levi and tangled with his heart as it tried to beat out of his chest. He slipped his hand lower, teasing the shorter hairs at Marsh's nape, and when Marsh shivered, Levi held him tighter. "I'm fine—" *Baby* was on the tip of his tongue, the endearment right there, natural and unprompted.

Terrifying.

Perhaps Marsh heard the unspoken word and was terrified of it too because his arms loosened, and he rolled back, giving them space. But giving Levi a cherished compliment in parting. "You're impressive is what you are."

Levi didn't care overly much about awards or commendations; he didn't hang them in his office or on his walls at home. He cared more about the respect of his peers, the approval of his bosses, and the love of his family. But the praise from Marsh made him preen more than a little, made him want to roll around in the security Marsh's words and arms offered.

Made Levi want to return the compliment. He paused at

the door, turning back with a smile. "You're impressive too. For a fucking cowboy."

Marsh's laugh echoed as Levi walked into the interrogation room with enough renewed confidence in his tank to ignore the body aches reasserting themselves.

"Mr. Beach, I'm Agent Kim," Matt said as Levi slid into the chair beside him. "This is Agent Bishop."

"I want a lawyer," Frederick said.

"You haven't been charged with anything."

"Though this bitcoin scheme you're running is something else," Levi said. "And not just for your friends at Celome."

Frederick's pale complexion went so ghostly he could've faded into the white walls. "I have no idea what you're talking about."

"How many off-book clients do you have?" Matt asked.

"Is it just Johnny and Orchard Investments?" Levi pressed.

Marsh piped into their ears. "ID'd two of the other sets. Camino cartel."

"How much money have you laundered for the Camino cartel?" Matt said.

"Better question..." Levi rested his forearms on the table. "How much have you *stolen* from them? We know you're skimming some for yourself. What do you tell them it is? A transaction fee? Do you tell them at all?"

"Or do you owe them for something else?" Matt swerved, a well-played detour judging by Frederick's audible gulp.

Levi followed him down the new road. "Is that why you went into business with Johnny? To skim enough to pay Camino back?"

"You know you'll never be able to pay them back," Matt said. "That's not how the cartels work."

The change of course and escalating pressure worked. "Look, I made some mistakes," Frederick said. "I'm trying to get out of them."

"By using your day job to rip off legit companies? What would your employer think?"

Realizing the door his slip had opened, Frederick pressed his lips together, not answering.

"Whose idea was it to rip off Celome?" Levi said.

"If it was Johnny's or Amanda's, maybe we can go easier on you," Matt offered.

Levi sweetened the deal. "If you give us what we need on Orchard, that could maybe reduce your time some more."

Frederick's gaze bounced between them, probably hoping for more give. Seeing none, he smartly decided to accept the deal on the table. He blew out a giant breath and propped his elbows on the metal table. "What do you need?"

The door opened, and Marsh appeared, a sheet of paper in hand. He handed it to Levi, then slipped back out. Levi scanned the scaled down version of their traffickers' funds flow.

"Who was that guy?" Frederick asked.

"Special Agent Marshall," Matt replied. "He's not very happy you tried to run his husband"—he tilted his head toward Levi—"over today."

Another audible gulp.

Levi pushed the sheet of paper across the table to Frederick. "Do these transactions look familiar?"

Frederick nodded. "Orchard."

"Is this payment"—he pointed to the one from last week —"for two transactions or are you skimming?"

Frederick's laugh was a harsh, disbelieving thing. "I'm not stupid enough to skim off Orchard. They're scarier than Camino."

"Where'd the leftover money go then?"

"Withers Transport."

In Levi's ear, fingers flew across keyboards, followed by Marsh's voice a moment later. "Withers has direct access to dozens of rail yards between here and Long Beach."

Great, more fucking rail yards. But it made sense. Easy transport for trafficking humans and illegal goods.

"When did you make that transfer?" Matt asked.

"I set it up today to cycle through bitcoin, then payout next Friday with an access code."

"What's the code?"

He rattled off a series of numbers, letters, and symbols that Marsh repeated back.

"Your contact has that code?" Levi asked, and Frederick nodded. "Do you have a name and number for your contact?"

"No name, just a number. It's on the cell phone you confiscated. Listed under George Washington."

"Real original," Marsh grumbled, and Levi suppressed a laugh. "This is good, Frederick," he said to their suspect. "Real good."

"Good enough I won't go to jail?"

"Good enough you won't go to the same jail where Orchard and Camino have people."

Frederick's bitter laugh returned, darkened by resignation. "Impossible." He hung his head in his hands, the picture of woe. "They're everywhere."

FOURTEEN

LEVI STOOD in his office doorway, shoulder against the jamb, trying and failing to be mad about the fact his desk had been commandeered. Not an ounce of anger could be found. Not with Marsh behind his desk, his shirt sleeves rolled up, his dark hair mussed, his contacts long gone and replaced by his sexy glasses. He was the epitome of rumpled handsome, made more so by the fact he'd worked as long and as hard as Levi had all day. He'd bounced between Levi's cases and his own, the call with Hong Kong keeping him at the office when Levi had left earlier for home and dinner with David. Now, three hours later, after a run, shower, and change into casual clothes for Levi, Marsh looked no closer to leaving than he had when Levi had first headed home. "You gonna stay here all night?"

Marsh didn't look up from the satellite photos spread across Levi's desk. "How late is it?"

"Closing in on nine."

"Shit." Later than he expected, then. He removed his

glasses, tossed them onto the photos, and pinched the bridge of his nose, eyes scrunched closed. "You didn't have to come back to get me. I've still got a few more hours of work."

"Follow-up on the Hong Kong call?"

He nodded. "Plus another call at midnight." He scrubbed his hands over his face, then stood. "I can do it from home, though."

Home.

Levi liked the way that sounded, liked that he could give Marsh that, but before they went home, he needed to give Marsh something else. "Let's get some food in you first."

They gathered Marsh's things, climbed into the RX, and made the short drive to Pacific Heights Brewing, a local craft brewery nestled among the mix of R&D, industrial, and office buildings that had joined Qualcomm in filling up Sorrento Valley.

"I thought you were taking me for food," Marsh said, "not a beer."

"Beer's good here. Food's even better." He pushed up his Henley sleeves and tilted his head toward the dining side of the facility. "And the Giants game is still on."

They checked in with the greeter, who led them to the outdoor beer garden, seating them at one of the picnic tables with a view of the bar and its crown of TVs, each one tuned to a different baseball game.

"Not a Padres fan?" Marsh said as he settled on the bench across from him. "Or the Dodgers or Angels?"

"Meh on the first. Fuck no on the second. Angels who?"

Marsh chuckled. "NL teams, got it."

"Kristin was from San Jose. Converted me to a Giants fan. And they're just more fun to watch."

As evidenced by the pitcher's homer into McCovey Cove, not the first tonight according to the stats at the bottom of the screen. Not much of a game either with the score already nine to one in the bottom of the seventh. Levi didn't mind; the man across from him was entertaining enough.

Marsh turned this way and that on his bench, glancing around in wonder. "This place is amazing."

"Isn't it?" The far edge of the beer garden was lined with fire pits and cozy lounge areas, picnic tables were arranged in the middle space, and the bar was situated at the other end, under the building's giant stone and metal overhang. Bistro lights were strung across the entire area, concentrated in the middle around the giant acacia tree that overhung much of the patio, giving the beer garden a cozy, magical feeling. "Credit to Matt," Levi said. "Dude doesn't go anywhere without a where-to-eat list, and PH Brewing was on his one for San Diego. I'd always enjoyed their beer, but they just recently opened the beer garden."

"Doesn't hurt it's close to the office."

"That too."

"Speaking of, did you get clearance—"

"Nuh-uh-uh." Levi gestured with his bar-towel-rolled utensils. "No shop talk over dinner." He unrolled the silverware and laid the towel across his lap. "That was Kristin's rule, and it was a good one. Between her cases and mine, it could get depressing."

"Fair enough." Marsh arranged his own silverware on either side of the oversized menu. "Tell me what's good here."

Food, beer, and sports talk passed the time until their server delivered Marsh's stout and Levi's IPA with their hummus platter and white pizza following soon after. Levi was halfway to his mouth with a piece of pie when Marsh's, "So, you're bi?" made him freeze midlift. "What?" Marsh said around a falafel ball. "You said no shop talk, and June's wedding is this weekend. I need to know more about you than that your favorite color is green and your insomnia rivals my own."

Levi doubted the question was half so innocent. He bit into the pizza and let his eyes flicker closed, enjoying the mix of cheeses, the earthiness of truffle oil, the sweetness of honey, and the last kick of crushed red pepper. When he opened his eyes again and met Marsh's darkened ones, he knew the question wasn't even half innocent. "You haven't picked up more around the house?"

"I have." Marsh loaded a piece of pita with hummus and chermoula and kept Levi in suspense while he made a mess eating it, satisfied groans and all. Payback was fucking torture.

"Well?" Levi prompted, snippier than intended.

Marsh snickered and licked his fingers clean. Fucker. Transfixed, Levi almost missed the start of Marsh's litany. "Let's see, I know how you take your morning tea and your oatmeal. That you start the week with a short run but add ten minutes each day. That you probably adopted Taco thinking he would run with you, but Kristin probably knew greyhounds are giant lapdogs and not-so-secretly laughed at your frustration."

He wasn't wrong. Taco rarely wanted to leave Kristin's lap, awkwardly sprawled across it as he was, in favor of a run with him. Definitely not a long one. *Short track racers, not marathon runners,* Kristin used to tease. That memory usually brought an ache to Levi's chest, but tonight, it only brought fondness. He rubbed a hand across his sternum, savoring the warmth.

Marsh tracked the movement, and when Levi didn't comment verbally, continued with his observations. "I also see you struggle to keep David motivated while also giving him the space he needs *and* how you stash ties everywhere around the house."

Levi finished his piece of pizza, washing down the last bite with a gulp of beer. "You've picked up a lot already."

"I'm still working out the details." He popped a dolma into his mouth. "Like whether you've ever acted on your attraction to men or if that's limited to internet porn?"

Levi downed the rest of his beer and signaled their server for another. He wasn't expecting this conversation tonight, but Marsh was right. June's wedding was in three days, and they would be expected to know these details about each other, no matter how quick the romance and no matter how private the information. Someone would ask, imply, or reference, and it wasn't fair to keep Marsh in the dark. "I prefer pan, and yes, I've been with people who identify as men before and with those who do not. You?"

"Gay," Marsh said. "And I've got no qualms about you being attracted to your own and other genders if that's even how attraction works for you." Levi cocked his head, not expecting the attraction qualifier. His surprise must have shown, Marsh smiling as he dunked a roasted carrot in whipped ricotta. "Brax's husband, Holt, identifies as demi and pan. Holt's family also runs queer teen shelters I help out at when I'm in town. I had to get up to speed if I wanted to understand and help those kids."

Was this guy for real? How many times had he listened to Kristin patiently explain demisexuality to family and friends? How many times had he listened to her fume afterward, in private, about someone who refused to accept the gray-ace spectrum and those on it? And now into his life walked this guy who just got it? Who'd made the active effort to learn?

Their server dropped off two more beers, and Marsh propped an elbow on the table as he tipped up his refreshed bottle. "So, then, how many guys have you been with?"

And poof, there went any extra credit Levi had just awarded him. "I'm not trading numbers with you."

Marsh grinned around the mouth of his bottle, and Levi guessed the question had been asked to needle him more than anything. Levi needled right back with the truth. "There were more men before Kristin. I'm attracted to all genders but had better luck with guys when I was younger, though even that was a challenge sometimes. Lots of assumptions were made about me, the multisport athlete, being a top-happy jock." His mind rewound through awkward high school and college hookups. "They couldn't be more wrong. It was even harder to find a woman who understood I also needed to be fucked to get off."

"But Kristin did?"

"What that woman could do with a dildo and a strap on..." Levi grinned, more of that earlier warmth and fondness filling his chest. "She was fucking spectacular."

Marsh laughed, full and rumbly, loud enough to capture the attention of others around them. He reined it in and lowered his voice. "I'm glad you found her."

"Me too."

"And after?"

Cluster fuck city. Or rather no good fuck city. He had tried to date, had even tried hookup apps with disastrous consequences. "It's hard to find folks who'll give me what I need. They see the badge, the body, and assume I'm some kind of alpha daddy."

Amusement fled Marsh's dark eyes, replaced by liquid heat, and his low voice was gravel rough. "That's not what you need."

Levi let his own gaze wander over the cowboy's broad shoulders, over biceps that tested the seams of his dress shirt, over his scruffy jaw and the big hand wrapped around a bottle of beer. Let his mind spin fantasies about Marsh's strong shoulders and arms holding him down, his big hand pumping his cock, his scruff leaving beard burn on the insides of his thighs. Levi shifted, spreading his legs under the table to give his stiffening dick more room. "No, it's not."

The chipper server appeared next to their table. "You need anything else?"

"Check, please," Levi said. As soon as the server left, Marsh reached a hand his direction. Levi drew his back, avoiding the contact that was sure to burn. "We said we'd keep this professional." His voice shook, giving him away.

Marsh slid a leg against his under the table, hot— fucking scalding—through layers of fabric. Levi shivered, his entire body a live wire of trembling want. But Marsh didn't press further, holding them in tension-soaked stasis until the server returned with their check. He shifted back on his bench, taking away the tempting heat, while Levi closed their tab. "Thank you for dinner," he said. "And for bringing me here. It was excellent."

"Least I could do for the case assist today."

Smirking, Marsh drew farther away, slinging one then the other leg over the bench as he stood. "Don't break the rule now."

"Sorry about that," Levi said, apologizing for breaking the *no shop talk at dinner* rule.

Marsh's reply came as they approached the car. "I don't think you are." He grasped Levi by the biceps and hauled him close, chest to chest, cheek to cheek, and Levi realized Marsh's comment had been about the other rule. The *keep things professional* one they both seemed hellbent on breaking. The body against Levi's hardened. "All you have to do is ask," Marsh rumbled, his beard tickling the corner of Levi's mouth, his lips right there for the kissing, closer than the chaste brush to the cheek at their wedding. "Ask, baby, and I'll give you what you need."

Levi wanted to. Desperately. Wanted to ask for a kiss and so much more. For Marsh's big body to rut against and manhandle his own, for a good hard fuck and a full night's sleep in Marsh's arms.

But before Levi could loosen the knot of desire strangling his vocal cords, Marsh released his arm and stepped back. "Let's get home. I'm supposed to be on with Hong Kong again at midnight."

A reprieve, involuntary yet necessary, wanted and yet… *Not* wasn't right, was a flat out lie. Shouldn't, maybe, but that seemed like more of a lie every day too. In any event, *can't* was the answer tonight. But what about tomorrow night? The weekend? All the other nights between now and when their cases were closed?

If the answer was yes on any of those nights—*when* it was yes, because as hard as his body still was, as hard as Marsh's had been against his, Levi didn't see how it wouldn't be yes eventually—would their sham of a marriage and everything they'd worked for the past two weeks go up in flames?

FIFTEEN

LEVI SAT at the kitchen island working and definitely not thinking about the man on the phone upstairs or how badly he still wanted to kiss him when David emerged from his cave. "Shouldn't you be asleep?" Levi said with a pointed look at the glowing 12:45 a.m. on the oven clock.

"Just finished a book." He grabbed a soda from the fridge. "Needed a drink."

"Not that one this late."

David pointedly eyed the soda next to Levi's laptop, an eerily spot-on reflection.

"Touché." Levi chuckled and closed his laptop. "Grab some cups, and I'll split it with you."

"I can live with that." He grabbed two red cups and filled each with ice.

"Making headway on that summer reading list?" Levi asked.

"Slowly."

"So not the book you were up late reading?"

"Definitely not." Levi raised a brow, and he answered

the unspoken question. "It was a book about chess. Strategies and stuff. Marsh gave it to me."

Levi hid his pleased smile behind the lip of his cup. "But you are still reading the others?"

"When I can." David circled the island and claimed the stool next to him. "Nicole's a tyrant. Clean the yoga studio top to bottom, David." His impression of his aunt was spot-on, right down to Nicole's excited head bobble while she asked you to do the worst thing on her to-do list in the cheeriest voice possible. "Inventory supplies, kiddo. Update these billion spreadsheets I've fucked up beyond all reason."

"Language," Levi chided without much reproach. He could only imagine how shoddy his sister's bookkeeping was. "She needs to hire someone." He'd been telling Nicole that for over a year, ever since her studio was featured online by a prominent local celebrity, and its membership had soared.

"Maybe in the fall, when she no longer has me to do it on the cheap. Thank God I negotiated Fridays off."

"It was the yoga studio or volunteer on base."

"I'll take my pennies of pay and Fridays off, thank you very much."

"Hey now." He nudged his son's shoulder. "Your grandpa served, your grandma worked on base, your aunt and two uncles do now, and so did I as a kid."

"The food and movies are cheap, and maybe I'd get upgraded to paid and it would be better than the studio, but"—he swirled the soda in his cup—"I might also look at some guy's ass wrong and get beat."

He said the last bit casually with a roll of his eyes, but it was far from a throw-away comment. Levi had to make sure David understood that. He set down his soda, removed David's from his hand, and angled toward his son. "You're always going to have to be careful regardless. That's not the way it should be, but it's the way it is. You know that, right?"

David nodded. "I know that, but I'm not gonna hide."

"I'm not asking you too. That'd be awfully hypocritical." Without thinking, he glanced up, toward the man in the office upstairs that he'd almost kissed. Twice.

When he lowered his gaze, David's green one was assessing. "But that's not real."

Marsh's words from last week floated through his head. Bore repeating to David, who also needed to hear them. "It might be"—he hedged his bets—"one day. With someone."

David covered his ears and babbled a litany of "Nopes."

Levi gently tugged his hands down. "David, listen—"

"When are you gonna tell Nonna? What are you gonna tell her? June's wedding is Saturday."

"One, I saw what you did there with the deflection."

He shrugged out of Levi's hold and reclaimed his soda. "Learned from the best."

Why had he and Kristin raised such a sharp kid? No help for it now, and truthfully, there was no one Levi liked matching wits with more. Kristin's legacy was alive and well and keeping him on his toes. "Two," he carried on, "your grandmother called today. She wants us all at their place for dinner tomorrow night."

David nearly spit out his drink. He set down the cup, soda sloshing over the rim, and raised both hands. "Wait a sec. I have *two* days of required family time this weekend?"

"Yes." He clasped the outside of David's shoulders. "For ten hours of the forty-eight this coming weekend, you are going to spend time with the family who loves you despite your surly disposition." He squeezed, then let his son go. "Get over it."

David grumbled curses into his cup.

"As for what we'll tell her," Levi said, "the same story we've told everyone else."

"That you and Marsh are actually married?"

"Who better to sell it than your grandmother *if* she believes it?"

David snickered. "*If* she doesn't kill you first."

Valid point. "I'm hoping she'll just be happy I have a date and be more concerned with besting Aunt Liz."

David snickered some more and rubbed his palms together. "I can't wait to see this."

"Oh, so now you want to go?"

He slid off the stool, grabbed Levi's glass, and downed it too.

"Hey!" Levi said now with reproach. "You drank all of it!"

"I'm gonna try some of those maneuvers from the book since you know, I'm missing at least ten hours this week-end." He paused at the foot of the stairs, hand around the newel, gaze flicking up. "He's still working?"

"His usual hours plus the ones here."

David shook his head and cast another glance Marsh's direction. "Didn't think it was possible for someone to work more than you."

Guilt wafted in the air, tinging the otherwise easy mood. "David—"

"Maybe he'd like a soda too."

Before Levi could say more, David disappeared down the hallway to his room, leaving Levi uneasy over where that conversation had wandered, but at least David's parting words were consideration for someone else. He was a good kid under the smart mouth and storm clouds.

Taking his son's advice, Levi grabbed a fresh can of soda and a cup of ice and headed up the stairs. He stood outside the office door, listening for Marsh's voice. Nothing, but he didn't want to barge in if Marsh was on camera. Holding the cup and can in one hand, he withdrew his phone with the other and tapped out a text to Marsh. **Are you on video?**

No, came the reply. **I'll go on Mute too.**

Levi pocketed the phone and gently pushed open the door. And was immediately glad he'd taken David's suggestion. Marsh looked beat. He set the drink on the edge of the desk. "Thought you might need this."

Marsh's exhausted expression softened, and with the added sexiness of the glasses, Levi seriously considered climbing onto his lap and taking the kiss he'd been fixated on for the past few hours.

Marsh's eyes darkened, his thoughts drifting a similar direction, but then an "Agent Marshall?" from the computer speakers stole his attention away again.

He toggled his earpiece and shot a wink over his shoulder. "I'm here. Apologies, my sexy new husband distracted me."

"Moi," Levi mouthed with a wink of his own.

Marsh's answering laugh distracted Levi from sleep. All night long.

SIXTEEN

MARSH SWUNG the front door open to see an expression on Agent Kim's face he'd never seen there before—pissed off. His sharp, clean-shaven jaw was clenched, his nostrils were flared, and streaks of red colored his fair cheeks. Not a good start, especially for what he and Levi planned to tell him.

Marsh stepped aside for Matt to enter and attempted to smooth things over. "Sorry about the detour this morning. There's breakfast in it for you."

"Good, since your Dunkin' sucks. Since when are there no powdered or cream-filled donuts? America runs on Dunkin', unless you live in PQ. What the actual fuck?"

It was the first rant—possibly the longest string of words—Marsh had ever heard from the typically upbeat agent. He pressed his lips together to keep from laughing.

"Go ahead. Laugh," Matt said, calling him on it. "I know I'm being ridiculous, but I lived in Boston long enough to be offended. My old partner would be livid. I'm channeling his indignation. All of it righteous."

Marsh let loose the bubbling laughter and closed the door behind him. "I can't promise donuts, but my mother's TexMex breakfast casserole will be ready in twenty." He and David had prepped two trays last night. David had taken one with him to the yoga studio, and the other had remained at the house for bribery purposes. Marsh was willing to pull out all the stops to get Matt on their side, including eggs, chorizo, poblanos, cheese, and Texas toast. "There's something else we need to show you first."

"Quickly," Matt huffed. "That casserole smells fucking delicious."

He led Matt upstairs to the office, then hung back in the doorway as Matt entered. Levi, in the office chair, gave him a cursory welcome nod, then rolled out of the way as the other agent circled the room.

Matt was a pro at hiding his expressive face in interrogations, but he didn't bother doing that with them. His eyes narrowed under pinched brows and a wrinkled forehead as he peered first at the whiteboards, then the computer monitors, trying to grasp what he was seeing. As pieces started to come together, his eyes grew wide as saucers and his jaw unclenched, mouth hanging open in surprise. When the final piece fell into place, he snapped his mouth shut, raked a hand through his black hair, and rounded on Marsh, eyes hard and color high on his cheeks. "You're the legat who fucked up our raid."

"I am."

He cut a glare at Levi. "And you knew each other? Since December?"

Levi shook his head. "We did not."

They'd debated how much to tell Matt—the entire truth or only a portion. Like with Johnny, Amanda, and Frederick, the more people who knew any secret, the harder it became to keep. But they trusted Matt, he was a good agent, and if the cause was just and well grounded, good partners had your back. Marsh had also checked him out through mutual contacts in San Francisco. More support for the impression Marsh had formed of Agent Kim. If he and Levi wanted to catch these assholes, they needed all hands on deck, read in, and on board, especially a top-notch agent like Matt.

By the look of him, though, Matt still needed some convincing. "Have you lost your mind?" he asked Levi.

"Possibly." Levi slowly rotated in the seat, arms spread. "But look how far we've gotten with his help."

Matt's gaze darted to Marsh, then back. "Except we wouldn't have needed it if he hadn't fucked up the first op."

"We would have." Levi folded his hands in his lap, and while the resignation in his voice still scraped across Marsh's nerves, the determination that had grown alongside it over the past two weeks was starting to heal the rough patches. "We would have stopped that one transport, but you heard Frederick. A second was already scheduled, and that's just one piece of a larger puzzle. It is so much bigger than we thought."

Matt took another slow trip around the room, stopping in front of the boards that hurt Marsh's heart the worst. "I remember this bombing. We lost an FBI agent. Vienna, right?"

"That's right," Marsh said, and when Levi held out his hand, Marsh stepped the rest of the way into the room to clasp it, accepting the offered comfort. "She was my boss and also a good friend and mentor."

Matt rotated, his gaze dropping first to his and Levi's clasped hands before returning to Marsh's face. Sincerity shone in his eyes and filled his voice. "I'm sorry for your loss."

"Thank you. I've been chasing the organization that supplied the money to the terrorists behind that bombing for three years."

"And you think our cases are connected?"

"Let us show you." Marsh used Levi's hand in his to haul him out of his chair, then settled in front of his laptops. He opened files, moved documents onto the larger monitors, and with Levi's help, walked Matt along two paths that led to the same place—Eder Capital. They showed him other examples of EC's activities around the globe, including EC's money laundering activities and the direct path of one such Camino cartel transaction. Drugs sold, cash laundered by EC through bitcoin and other investments, three times as much back to Camino, a quarter used to buy weapons from the Bratva, facilitated by EC, a quarter used to fund more drug and human trafficking operations also facilitated by EC, a quarter used to bribe government officials, and the final quarter directly into the cartel king's offshore investment accounts, managed by... Eder Capital. It was all connected with EC taking its cut at every step from the criminals and criminal transactions it dealt with on a daily basis.

The last piece of the puzzle they showed Matt was the one Marsh had discovered yesterday, the one that had convinced them it was time to read Matt in. Marsh first opened the surveillance photo from the truck stop Matt and Levi's team had examined last week. Then he opened several similar photos from other trafficking handoffs, some from their files and others Marsh had found. In all of them, the same giant man with neck and forearm tattoos, his back always to the camera, was facilitating the transfer. "You recall your unsub."

"He's always there," Matt said, "managing the handoff of the trafficking victims."

Marsh opened a grainy photo from an ATM camera. He'd triangulated its position using stoplight cams and other surveillance cams at one of the additional exchange sites he'd identified. He sped the blurry photo through resolution cleanup until the program arrived at the face the recognition software had pinged. White with close-cropped brown hair and bushy dark brows prominent over sunken eyes, a nose that looked like it had been broken a time or twenty, and a hard mouth surrounded by a scruffy beard that covered the man's square jaw. "His name is Stefan Sanders. He immigrated here from Vienna with his family when he was eight. Three guesses who he has ties to."

"Fuck." Matt rested against the one swath of wall that didn't have something taped or pinned to it. "Eder Capital."

"His uncle, Charles Sanders, is the CEO," Levi said. "There seems to have been a falling out between Stefan's parents and Charles, but both Stefan and his sister, Catherine, are on Eder's payroll."

"Stefan for overseeing their investments, clearly." Matt folded his hands on top of his head. "What's his sister's role in all this?"

"Still trying to sort that out," Marsh said. "She works for an investment firm in London but frequently visits the US."

"Laundering," Matt said.

"Likely," Levi agreed. "We're still digging."

"All right," Matt said as he pushed off the wall. "I'm in."

Levi straightened where he stood next to Marsh. "Just like that?" They'd both been hopeful Matt would play ball, and they'd worked hard putting things together and deciding how to present the case, knowing this would be the first of many times they'd have to do it, the first of many people they'd have to convince, but even Marsh was surprised at Matt's swift buy-in.

"This is our job," Matt said. "This is also why we have legats and interagency cooperation. Crime rarely happens in a bubble. I learned that working kidnapping cases. Yes, many of those cases were tied to domestic disputes, but drugs and debt were often involved. I also saw enough kids illegally trapped and transported, including people close to me, to know how these trafficking systems work and why they have to be stopped. It's why I requested this assignment. So what's the plan?" He put his waving hands back on his head as if he was holding in more.

What Marsh had heard was enough. He looked to Levi, who likewise gave him a go-ahead nod. "Our plan is to attack Eder's foundation here in the States, their capital and supply, starting with your case."

"We intercept the next transport," Levi said, "and we cut off the flow of victims and funds."

The corner of Matt's mouth twitched, the agent fighting a smirk. "Using Frederick."

Marsh didn't bother to hide his. "Exactly."

"We get the evidence to tie EC to this," Levi continued. "And we also force them to make a different move, to show their hand. I want them on their heels, scrambling like we've been for the past eighteen months, and that's when we strike."

Marsh wanted to reach out again and clasp Levi's hand. Hell, any part of him. He wanted to feel the confidence and determination that vibrated in his words and around him. But before he even got around to the mental debate of whether he should, his phone on the desk vibrated with an incoming text.

"It's from Kwan," Marsh said as he read the message. "She wants to see me ASAP."

Levi and Matt exchanged a glance, then turned their gazes to him, the foreboding stares aimed back at him the same feeling that had settled in his own gut. Whatever she wanted, it couldn't be good.

SEVENTEEN

"YOU WANTED TO SEE ME?" Marsh said, closing Kwan's office door behind him.

She gestured at the visitor chairs across from her. "Levi updated me," she said as Marsh slid into one. "Seems he's caught a break on two cases."

"That's right." On their way in, he'd driven while Levi had called to brief the ASAC—on speaker. "I'm happy for him."

Kwan opened her mouth like she was about to lay into him, then pressed her lips together, inhaled a long slow breath, and proceeded with a forced calm that reminded Marsh so much of Brax he almost called her on it. She'd picked up a lot from her first CO at Camp Casey. "There are a half dozen cyber agents a floor up, and none of them have seen hide nor hair of you, and none of them helped Agent Bishop break a bitcoin laundering case."

He removed his hat and rested it on his crossed knees. "Bitcoin is a new favorite tool of transnational organized crime. It's on every legat's radar. I might have mentioned it to him."

"If you actually want to reside in this office, this is not the way to go about it."

"I want to do my job."

Arms crossed, expression grim, she leaned back in her chair, not buying the shit he was shoveling at all.

"I know you, Kwan. You're a results soldier. So long as the mission gets done, the cases get closed—"

"You forget there's an *assistant* at the front of my title." She spun half-around, grabbed a folder off the credenza, then tossed it onto the corner of her desk nearest him. "SAC Bell requests your assistance on a case."

"But I need—"

"You need to repair your image with the decision-makers in this office."

He couldn't argue with that mission either, not if he wanted to st—

He hit the brakes on thoughts of a long-term future he wasn't supposed to be contemplating and grudgingly snatched the file off the desk. Short term, he needed to stay in Kwan's and Bell's good graces long enough to close Levi's trafficking case and make headway on his own against EC. He flipped through the file... and snorted. "A junior cyber agent could handle this."

"Then *you* should be able to do the job quickly." A smile threatened, the soldier he knew breaking through. He, Levi, and Matt were in a position to move two cases off her board. He just had to appease the SAC and deal with this identity theft matter first. "You have a meeting with Bell in ten," Kwan said. "And put on a goddamn tie before you go in there."

"You think I have one?" Marsh said on the way to his feet.

"Borrow your husband's. And lose the hat too."

"I think you're secretly enjoying this."

"Nine minutes."

He was still chuckling as he ducked into Levi's office on his way to the elevator. "You got what you need to track accounts and transports?"

"Team's already on it. Why?"

"Your SAC wants me on an identity theft case." He dropped the file and his hat in one of the visitor chairs, freeing his hands to rummage through the garment bag that lived on the back of Levi's office door. "Kwan says I need a tie."

"She's not wrong, but you won't find one in there. Ketchup attack last week." He unknotted the paisley blue one around his neck, slid it out from under his collar, and tossed it across the desk to Marsh. "Bell's old school."

"And I'm career military." He looped the tie around his neck, tucked it under his collar, and tried to remember how to knot it.

"He's also racist and homophobic."

"Again, career military." Foiled by the slippery silk, he tried again. "I also grew up brown and gay in Texas. Tell me something I don't know how to handle."

"A tie apparently." Levi circled the desk to stand in front of him and made quick—close—work of the shiny strip of fabric.

"Once I took off the uniform, I banished these things."

"Fair." Before Levi could step back, Marsh reached out and flicked open the button of his collar. He didn't need to keep it buttoned with the tie gone. Flicked open another.

Levi gasped, a wobbly stuttered thing, and it was all Marsh could do not to slide a hand under Levi's collar and—"Just tread carefully."

About Bell or about the heat bubbling between them? Same answer, Marsh suspected. He stepped back before temptation ruined the only tie in the room. "Best behavior. Promise." He grabbed the file and tucked it under his arm. "If you get stuck, call Brax."

Levi hitched a hip on the edge of his desk, looking effortlessly handsome. "You're not the only cyber agent in the building."

"I'm the only one I trust. Call Brax if you get stuck. He'll get Holt or one of Redemption's other hackers on it."

"Okay, I'll call Brax. If it comes to that." He slid off the desk, snatched up Marsh's hat, and flipped it onto his head. Fuck the tie that had set off his blue eyes; Marsh liked the cowboy hat look on him even better. "And remember, we have to be out of here at four to pick David up and head to PB."

"See?" Marsh tapped his knuckles against the doorjamb. "SAC Bell is the least of today's worries."

⚜♟♟♟♟♟♟⚜

MARSH STOOD in front of the closed door a floor up from Kwan's office and ran two fingers inside his collar, trying and failing to loosen the obnoxious binding. He was not made for ties and had happily packed his away with this uniform. He'd knelt by his father's grave last year in a T-shirt, jacket, and jeans, and sworn on his mother's rosary that he was done putting on ties to try to impress people, like his father, who would never see past his brown skin or sexual orientation. Yet here he was again, putting on a tie to try to impress another old white guy. It had never worked with his father; why would it work with SAC Bell? At least this tie smelled like TexMex casserole and peppermint tea. He adjusted it a final time and knocked.

"Come in," a deep voice called.

He opened the door and stepped inside, unsurprised to find that Special Agent in Charge Bell's office looked like ninety percent of the SAC offices Marsh had been in. The walls were covered with plaques and certificates, the cabinet tops were littered with framed pictures and etched crystal things, and an obligatory family photo sat perched on the corner of his desk.

The SAC himself was standard-fare older white guy, maybe a bit fitter than the average SAC, but this was San Diego. Given his trim build, blond hair, and the smell of saltwater in the air, Marsh guessed he either surfed or ran by the ocean every morning. "You must be Agent Marshall," he said, a faint Midwestern twang to his voice. "I'm SAC Bell. It's a pleasure to meet you." He gave Marsh a once-over, then smiled, politician perfect, as he extended his hand. "Not at all what I expected based on the warnings."

"I like to surprise." He shook the other man's hand. "Thank you for your office's hospitality."

"Anything for a fellow army man."

"You served?" Marsh asked while mentally recataloguing the room. He didn't recall any military medals among the other law enforcement recognitions.

"I did a tour in Germany."

Ah, a short-timer. "It's lovely there," he answered with a

political smile of his own. One useful skill he'd learned from his father.

"You don't want to go back?" Bell asked. "To Europe?" He gestured at the visitor chairs, then circled behind the desk.

Marsh claimed a chair and forced himself not to fiddle with the tie. "If it's a choice between Europe and my husband, I'll take my husband."

Bell squirmed in his seat. "Of course. Love does make us do irrational things."

Marsh could counter that dig a million ways from Sunday, but Kwan's warnings—Levi's too—rattled around in his head. If he wanted to get back to helping his husband, he needed to play nice. For now. He removed the folder from under his arm. "Maj—Agent Kwan—said you needed my help with this identity theft case."

"Ah, yes, one of my contacts on the Hill is particularly interested in the outcome. I wanted our best cyber agent on it."

"Well, thank you, sir, but you have cyber agents on your team already who are more than capable and who have been with the Bureau longer."

"Come on, Agent Marshall." He leaned forward, a predatory gleam in his dark eyes that made the collar around Marsh's neck feel even tighter. "Your reputation precedes you."

Trap, his mental warning systems blared. There was definitely more to this than a fake ID. Maybe if he handled it quickly, he could avoid getting stuck in whatever mess was seeping his direction. "I took a brief look at the file. I should be able to make some headway."

"Excellent." Bell stood, and Marsh followed suit. "We thank you for it."

He'd almost escaped, his hand on the doorknob, when the truth revealed itself. "Oh, and Agent Marshall, if you wish to stay in this office with your husband, Representative Anthony's son is not to be implicated in whatever you might find."

EIGHTEEN

FOLLOWING David along the terra-cotta path to his parents' front door, Levi experienced a rush of insecurity. Not about the obvious—the fact that he'd married Marsh without his mother present—but about what the cowboy by his side would think of his childhood home. It was smaller than the house in PQ. Older and quirkier. A funky flow inside and even funkier on the outside with desert orange stucco, a red tile roof, decorative tiles around the windows, and an arched front door with a sun carved into the wood. It was the type of house you'd expect his once-a-hippie mother to call home, a radical departure from the military bases where she and his father had worked. A perfect escape for them and their family, the epitome of love and whimsy and acceptance, and the perfect retirement oasis for the bohemian beach bums they'd become. It was the polar opposite of Aunt Liz's sprawling Rancho Sante Fe mansion where June's wedding would be held the next day.

"You're awfully quiet," Marsh said.

"You have been too. Is it work or nerves?"

"Me? Work." He held a bouquet of flowers in one hand and adjusted his hat with the other. "You?

"Nerves," Levi admitted. "Are you gonna tell me about the meeting with Bell?" There were work nerves for Levi too, mixed in with the meet-the-parents ones. After his meeting with Bell, Marsh had returned Levi's tie, and Levi had offered him his office since he'd be in the war room with his team. *Too tempting*, Marsh had said, then disappeared to his assigned desk with the other cyber agents, only returning when it was time to leave.

"One battle at a time," Marsh said with a sideways smile that widened when Amy opened the front door, her ten fingers spread. "Is she scoring my outfit?"

Ten points seemed too little for Marsh's bright white Stetson, matching dress shirt with an open collar and rolled sleeves, dark jeans, and a shiny belt buckle and boots. But, sadly, that wasn't the meaning of Amy's jazz hands. "It's our signal for code red."

"Code red?"

"Mom's trying to set me up," Levi explained.

"Ohmigod." David cackled. "It just keeps getting better."

"Watch it," Marsh playfully warned as he and Levi joined David and Amy inside the gated courtyard. "I will whoop your ass at chess tomorrow morning."

"If you haven't been murdered first." Snickering, David scooted past them, veering left through another gate and around the house to the patio and backyard where Levi heard the rest of his family.

Marsh leaned close, whispering conspiratorially. "He can never meet Helena Madigan."

"You know he's gay, right?" Just this morning, there'd

been a heated debate over which Bond was hottest. Levi had been voted off the island for even suggesting Roger Moore be in the top three.

"Yes," Marsh said with a smirk. "I know, and Helena is in her midthirties and happily married to a woman, but those two in the same room would set off a snark explosion that would kill us all." He stepped from Levi's side to Amy's, bending to kiss her cheek. "Amy, good to see you again."

She blushed and smiled for Marsh, swooning in a way that would never not be hilarious on her, but her amusement quickly vanished when she turned her dark-eyed glare on Levi. "You should have at least told Mom you were bringing a date."

Levi cringed. "How bad is it?"

"On a scale of one to ten, about a six."

"That's not terrible," Marsh said.

"I'm pretty sure Renée is more interested in my wife than she'll ever be in either of you, but Mom's grasping at straws."

Marsh angled his direction. "It's really that important to her that you have a date for this wedding?"

He probably should have spent more time this morning filling Marsh in on the Morelli sisters and less time lobbying for Roger Moore, but alas, hot Bond debates were more enjoyable. "Mom and Aunt Elizabeth were born nine months apart."

"But they weren't close?"

"Oh, they were besties... until they weren't. Puberty kicked in, everything became a competition, and here we are, fifty years later."

It only took a second for Marsh's eyes to grow big and

his jaw to drop, the light bulb going off. "Wait, Margaret and Elizabeth? Were they named after the British royals?"

"Yep," Amy said. "It's like Grandma Morelli set them up to battle forever." Amy slapped the back of his shoulder. "Now you can try to lasso them, Cowboy. The flowers are a good start. Bring smaller ones to the wedding for Aunt Liz."

Before Marsh could comment, the gate to their left swung open and an attractive woman Levi didn't recognize appeared in the courtyard. "Oh, you must be Levi." She extended a hand and a kind, easy smile. "Hi, I'm Renée. Can you apologize to your mom for me? I just got a call from a coworker that, not gonna lie, I've crushed on for years. She was stood up by a date and needs a shoulder to cry on."

"No worries." Levi opened the gate for her to exit. "I hope it works out for you."

Marsh doffed his hat and drawled, "Good luck."

Renée dramatically swooned against the gate, a hand splayed over her chest. "Ugh, if I liked dick."

"I know, sweetie," Amy added. "Said the same thing the first time I met him."

Renée's gaze shot to Amy, and she seemed to swoon for real at the casual endearment. "If it doesn't work out with me and Sheila, you and Courtney game for a third?"

"Could be." Amy's smile was more seductive than Levi ever wanted to see. "She give you our numbers?"

Renée nodded.

"Good luck, then, with a caveat."

Renée skipped down the path, a winner either way, and so was Levi's sister. "Did you just pick up my date?"

"It appears I did."

Marsh hip-checked him. "One skirmish won."

"Don't get cocky, Cowboy," Amy warned. "The battle's just begun."

Instead of going around the house, Amy led them through it, and Levi's nerves returned. The many decades of furniture, decorations, and technology were eclectic at best, haphazard at worst, a minefield for a guy as big as Marsh to navigate, but he managed it well. He swerved from the path Amy cut to take a closer look at the dining room walls covered in family photos. "I know it's tight and cluttered," Levi said, trying to distract him before he reached the awkward middle school years.

Marsh rotated in the narrow space between the wall and table, surveying again the living area they'd walked through. "It's perfect."

"Perfect?"

"Reminds me of the ranch back home. Jefferson, my dad, was a rich white guy. Family connections and old money. Sowed his wild oats for a while at UT. That's where he met Mom. He went to law school, decided to become a professor, got on tenure track and back on track with his family's expectations."

"Which didn't include your mom?"

"Especially not my mom and especially not her *flaunting* her Mexican heritage. So when she left him, she flaunted it, loudly, all around the ranch he paid for with a sizable divorce settlement."

Levi tried to smother his laughter, then spit it out when Marsh slapped him on the back. "It's funny. Go ahead. Mom laughs about it every day." Levi let go of his nerves, carried away on laughter that felt good and easy.

Until another voice joined them from the patio door.

"Well, that's a welcome—" His mother's words died when Amy stepped aside and gave her a clear view of him and Marsh. "What's this?"

"Hey, Mom." Levi stepped forward, wrapping her in a hug and kissing the crown of her head, the brown and silver curls tickling his nose. She tolerated it for all of two seconds, then shifted so she could see around him, eyeing the giant stranger in her living room.

Marsh removed his hat and held out the bouquet. "Ma'am, these are for you."

She accepted the bouquet but not without suspicion. "Who are you?"

"Mom," Levi said as he moved back beside Marsh. "This is Emmitt Marshall." He took a big, deep breath and clasped Marsh's hand. "My husband."

NINETEEN

"YOUR *WHAT*?"

Margaret's outburst was so loud, so sharp, that everyone around the patio farm table spun to see what was going on. Everyone except David, who laughed and flopped into a nearby camp chair.

Next to Marsh, Levi stood stock still, crushing his hand.

"Come on, Mom." Amy turned her by the shoulder toward the patio. "He should only have to tell his story once."

"Did you know about this?" Margaret demanded. Amy's silence was answer enough. Margaret shook off her hand and marched forward, arms spread wide, flowers losing half their petals as she whipped them around dramatically. "Well, you can all stop worrying about your brother now. He's married some cowboy and only your sister and David attended the wedding."

"Oh, I didn't go," David piped up unhelpfully.

Margaret rounded on Levi. "Your own son wasn't at your wedding?" The speed at which she crossed the patio back to him and swatted him with the bouquet was impressive. "What's wrong with you?"

Having sat on the sidelines long enough and desperately needing blood flow to his hand, Marsh entered the fray. "I believe this is my fault, ma'am," he said, laying the accent on thick.

"This should be good," David muttered.

Marsh mentally calculated how few moves he needed to beat him at chess tomorrow morning.

The man with a thick head of silvery blond hair at the head of the table stood. "And who are you?"

Marsh recognized Captain Tom Bishop from photos here and at Levi's house. "Colonel Emmitt Marshall." He extracted his hand from Levi's, handed Levi his hat, then held out a hand to Levi's father. "It's a pleasure to meet you, Captain."

Tom's grip was firm but not overly so. "Which branch, Colonel?"

"Army, retired several years back. I spent most of my time at Camp Casey in Afghanistan."

"Front line?"

"Yes, sir." He didn't have to call Tom sir—technically Marsh was the higher rank—but he was his elder, his husband's father, and, by his rank, a leader in whatever unit he'd served. "Cyber warfare and tactical field support. I'm with the FBI now, stationed at The Hague."

"Did you meet at work?" Margaret asked behind them.

"Yes and no." Marsh angled so he could speak to both of them. "One of my best friends, a retired Lieutenant Colonel and a former chief of police, lives in San Francisco. I did some work out of the field office there when I was in town."

"Levi," Nicole said from the table. "You were there last winter, right?"

"That's when we met." Levi joined him beside the table. "We've kept things quiet since we're both with the Bureau."

Margaret didn't look convinced. "That's allowed?"

"Technically, yes. But we didn't want to say anything until we knew for sure our jobs weren't in jeopardy."

They were, but not for the reasons anyone here suspected. Marsh met Tom and Margaret's gazes, then swept his own over the rest of Levi's family gathered around the table, selling the reason that mattered here. "I didn't want Levi to upset any of you if this was over before it had barely begun."

"Don't forget the best part," David said. "He's loaded."

Fucking teenagers. If Levi wasn't still holding his hat, Marsh would've chucked it at his son.

Levi's *"David!"* was the verbal equivalent, but it wasn't enough to shut the teenager up.

"What? It's true!"

"And rude," Amy added, swatting him with her hand like Margaret had done to Levi with the flowers.

Speaking of Margaret, she was not done speaking. "But did you have to get married?"

"Mom," Levi groaned, and Marsh almost chuckled at the many layers of embarrassment in the one word. "Also rude."

"Runs in the family," David commented, and Levi did throw Marsh's hat at him then. It hit him right in the forehead. Bull's-eye.

Marsh couldn't hold in the laughter any longer. "Rude and blunt are two different things." Smiling, he looped an arm around Levi's shoulders, tugging him closer. "And yes, as soon as I knew we were in the clear, I hauled him off to the courthouse. I didn't want to wait another second to marry him."

Dual sighs rang out from the other end of the table. That was Nicole and Bella sold.

Now Levi just had to close the deal with his mother. "I also didn't want to overshadow June's wedding," he told her. "I know you and Aunt Liz. You'd want to best her, and I've already had the best wedding. After going through mine, all of ours"—he gestured around the table at his sisters—"and her own siblings' weddings, June deserves to be the center of attention."

Tom bumped shoulders with his wife. "He's got a point, M."

She cut an appreciative glance at her husband, and when she looked back his and Levi's way, there was a calculating glint in her eye, one Marsh had seen in David's over the board before. "But you're bringing him to the wedding, right?" she asked.

"I wouldn't miss it," Marsh answered.

She nodded, then, as if a thought had suddenly occurred to her, looked past them toward the courtyard. "Where'd Renée go?"

"To meet the woman she would like to marry," Amy said.

"Ooh, oops." Margaret giggled, and there was the smiling happy woman Marsh had seen in all the family photos, the strong-willed, big-hearted mother who'd raised four bright kids, two who had won Marsh over already. "Well, worked out anyway." She sniffed the bouquet still in her hands, winked at Marsh, then spun and set her sights on Levi's sister at the other end of the table. "Now, Nicole, about Maddie..."

Marsh eavesdropped on Margaret's wedding dos and don'ts for children for several seconds before his attention was snatched away by Levi's relieved sigh.

"Well, that went about as well as I expected," Levi mumbled.

Using the arm around his shoulders, Marsh pulled him closer and kissed his temple. "Way to rip off the Band-Aid, babe."

Levi looped an arm around his waist, leaning into him, and Marsh was more than happy to lend his strength. But the satisfying moment only lasted a second. Levi tensed as if realizing he'd given away too much, but as Marsh looked down at him, then followed his line of sight to where David sat unnaturally still, watching them, his green eyes narrowed, Marsh felt the specter of the past rise up between them.

A reminder that no matter how much Levi leaned on him, no matter how comfortable they became around each other, no matter how much heat built between them, and no matter how well they sold this to friends and family, Levi was still emotionally unavailable.

Was still in love with his late wife.

Marsh gave Levi one more squeeze, then dropped his arm and put a few feet between them. He clapped and rubbed his hands together, drawing Margaret's attention. "Now, where's this beef and cheddar lasagna I've heard so much about?"

His appetite was gone, but he'd fake it, would continue to sell this and continue to fall harder for Levi and his family because that was his curse and what he deserved.

TWENTY

"I THINK it's safe to say all is forgiven with my mother." Levi slid his tie out from under his shirt collar and tossed it onto the back of the couch with Marsh's discarded jacket and hat.

Across the kitchen, Marsh was already in the liquor cabinet, pulling down the whiskey and vermouth. "I don't think I've ever seen anyone as gleeful over another person's shock."

Levi couldn't say he'd ever seen his mother so pleased either as when he, Marsh, and David had arrived for the wedding, and she'd introduced her new son-in-law to Aunt Liz. "It was everything Mom's ever wanted." He reached into the freezer, grabbed the satchel of whiskey cubes, then snagged two glasses out of the drying rack on his way to Marsh's side. "You tipped that hat, did your thing, and poor Aunt Liz was a goner. I guarantee she's already plotting how to lure you to her side of the family."

As soon as the words were out, Levi realized he shouldn't have said them. He'd forgotten for a moment, for an evening, that this was all an act that would end sooner rather than later. But this arrangement between him and Marsh hadn't felt like an act today; it had felt like relief. He didn't have to stand there alone and weather the looks of pity he'd grown accustomed to the past two years. There was no room for sadness in the face of shock and awe, in sheer hilarity on more than one occasion. Marsh had charmed them all, Levi most of all, hovering by his side, never more than a few feet away, making sure it was clear whose date he was, who he belonged to. And he'd relished in telling the story of their whirlwind romance, the two of them settling into an easy narrative rhythm, finishing each other's sentences and spinning a tale folks swooned over.

Yet, as Marsh diligently stayed in Levi's orbit, he also diligently kept a discreet distance between them. Levi had noticed it last night, had felt it like a physical thing. Was Marsh just being careful not to set off David's alarm bells again? Or was there something else? It was both comforting —he needed the distance as a reminder—and confusing— he wanted Marsh, plain and simple, and the distance was in the fucking way.

Hence his slip of the tongue, his subconscious trying to steal a few more minutes in the land of make believe. Marsh thankfully slid into it with him, playing along instead of giving him a hard time. Or worse, adding to the distance. "Who's Aunt Liz got left?" he asked as he mixed up Manhattans in the crystal Yarai.

"No one. All her kids are married now." Levi divided the whiskey stones between the glasses and pushed them in front of Marsh, who poured in the cocktail. "But I don't think that would matter much to her in your case."

Marsh's laugh boomed around the kitchen. "I think I like the more love, less glam side of the family."

"Cheers to that." Levi lifted his glass, and they clinked rims.

"I didn't expect so much security at a family wedding."

"One of Liz's kids is a rock star. He didn't show, though."

"That what bought the big house behind those iron gates?"

"No, that was all Aunt Liz's husband." As they continued to chat, Levi checked once more on Taco and Burrito who were curled together on the game room couch and texted David **Good night**, assuming he would break from the marathon gaming session with Bella's kids at some point. "Still not sure exactly what he does, but it pays well."

"Your cousin was great about it all, the extra security and us."

"That's June." Levi pocketed his phone, retrieved his glass, and led Marsh outside to the club chairs on either side of the patio fire pit. "She's had to roll with the punches more than anyone. I'm glad she got a good one, finally, and a gloom-free evening for her wedding." The morning marine layer had burned off early, leaving behind a sunny afternoon and pleasant evening. Nearing midnight now, the mist had crept back in, snaking through the canyon and chilling the air. Perfect weather for an after-party drink by the fire. He flicked it on, then sank back in the chair.

"Do you think they bought it?" Marsh said.

Levi didn't have to ask what, Marsh still mulling over Levi's earlier slip too. "Mom bought it and sold it hard. To everyone." She'd corralled them as soon as they'd walked through the leaded-glass doors, taken them immediately to Aunt Liz, then spent the rest of the evening bringing every relative and family friend by for an introduction. It had taken an act of God—and Amy's interference—to steal ten minutes uninterrupted with June and her new husband. "It was like she had a beacon on us and a checklist of everyone we needed to see."

Marsh chuckled. "I did worry the jig was up when I told her I didn't dance."

"Promising to let her teach you was a nice save." He sipped his cocktail, debating whether to poke at a curiosity that had bugged him all night, then went for it. "I'm surprised you don't dance. I thought you knew how to do everything."

"Flatterer." Marsh leaned toward the fire, elbows propped on his knees. "And I do know how to dance."

"Then why—"

"Because if I danced with her, I'd have to dance with you."

A scoff was on the tip of Levi's tongue—he could dance, well enough not to step on a single one of Marsh's toes, not that he'd feel it anyway through those shiny boots—but then Marsh angled his face, gaze cutting Levi's direction, and the flicker of fire in his dark eyes wasn't only a reflection of the pit's flames.

Oh.

The realization incinerated Levi's indignation. Yes, dancing with Marsh would have been a problem. Dangerous even. Their bodies closer than either had allowed since last night, since earlier that week in the brewery parking lot. Chest to chest, arms around each other, lips close enough—

A coyote's howl cut through Levi's spiraling thoughts. As did Marsh's nonreaction. "You don't startle at them."

Marsh turned his face back to the fire and downed another gulp of cocktail. "When I retired from the army, I didn't think I wanted to live anywhere like the desert. No more searing heat, no more grimy sand." A second coyote's call joined the first, and Marsh smiled. "No more howling dogs, of one sort or another. I'd been in Afghanistan almost half my life, in Texas the other half. Wanted to try something different."

"That's how you ended up at The Hague."

Marsh nodded. "I went from all the sand to all the water. Kwan had introduced me to Sophie, and after working several joint ops, I wanted to work with her officially." Marsh's voice grew softer, thicker, as he spoke of his late friend and former boss. Levi reached out and laid a hand in the crook of his elbow. Marsh covered it with his own and held it there, taking the comfort Levi offered. "It's nice there, the change was good, but the part of me that connects with the land and my roots feels more at home in the desert—in a place like this—than in the Netherlands."

"Tell me about it."

"The Netherlands?"

"No, home." Levi withdrew his hand, reclaimed his own glass, and sat back in his chair. Marsh spoke fondly of his moms and home but rarely in detail. There was the nugget about the bougainvillea, the delicious casserole, the comparisons to Levi's own childhood home, but nothing else so concrete. Levi wanted more. "Tell me about the ranch your asshole father paid for."

Marsh smiled and tossed back his last gulp of Manhattan. "It's in West Texas." He set the empty glass on the fire pit ledge. "The family that owned the property had a small cattle operation, a hunting license, and a two-thousand-square-foot casita."

Two thousand square feet was almost as large as the house ten feet behind them. "That's a little bigger than a *casita*."

"Compared to their megamansion in San Antonio, our house was a casita."

"Did your mom know anything about ranching?"

"She grew up on a ranch in El Paso," Marsh answered. "When she left for Austin, Camilla García swore she'd never go back to the desert."

Like mother, like son. "But the desert called to her too?"

"It's the García blood. She's also a conservationist and card-carrying member of the Sierra Club. The chance to run an environmentally conscious ranch and to turn the excess acreage into a wildlife preserve were the ultimate fuck-you to my father and hers. Ranching the right way, that's her motto. She brought Irina on as her gamekeeper, fell madly in love with her, and that's how I got two wild and crazy moms."

It sounded idyllic and chaotic at the same time. Similar in ways to Levi's own childhood, despite the obvious differences. Whimsical and full of love, once Marsh's parents had divorced. "What was it like growing up there?"

"Easy and hard at the same time. Mom and Irina supported anything I wanted to do—football, chess club, computer club, rodeo—"

Levi lurched in his chair. "Wait! Rodeo? You're a *real* cowboy?"

"Been roping most of my life feels like. Did it competitively all through middle and high school. First place at the state finals three years in a row." He jutted a thumb over his shoulder, back toward the house. "I had to learn how to wear that hat. Earn it."

"Jesus." Levi could barely stand within three feet of a horse. He'd fallen off one when he was four—in the very canyon below them—and had never gotten over it. He was terrified of the beasts. He couldn't imagine riding one while roping cattle, or wrestling a steer, or hanging on for dear life while it tried to bounce you off. He shivered at the thought and scooted closer to the fire. He wasn't surprised that Marsh had run straight at those challenges. It made a certain amount of sense with how quickly he thought on his feet and how well he could wrangle anyone to his side.

How well Marsh had wrangled him.

How he *could* wrangle him in a different context.

Levi had been out to the rodeo in Ramona once when he was in college. He remembered the steer wrestling event in particular. Recalled how with enough strength, perfect timing, and the right leverage, a cowboy could wrestle a bull into submission. He'd had a hard-on that entire night, had never wanted to be a steer so badly in his life. Now, years later, sitting next to a smart and devastatingly handsome cowboy, his eyes dark and skin aglow in the light of the fire, Levi's pants were becoming tight all over again, the fantasy a thousand times more potent.

"Whatever it was, though," Marsh continued, dragging Levi out of the fantasy and back to the present, "Mom and Irina expected me to be the best at it. They were both kids of immigrants, Mom's from Mexico, Irina's from Poland, and that *I have to be better so I can stay* mentality was always there, pushing them and pushing me."

"Is that why you joined the military?"

"In part. I was recruited while I was at UT."

"Cyber?"

He nodded. "I was a computer science major with a political science minor. Wrote my senior thesis on cyber warfare."

"I bet they snatched you right up."

"My CompSci adviser was married to one of the ROTC instructors. Cyber was becoming an obvious need, and then after 9/11, we became the front line."

"And you wanted to be the best."

Marsh smirked, but it wasn't his usual charming one. This one was bitter and self-deprecating, and it looked so unnatural and uncomfortable on him that Levi scooted back in his chair. "I thought it was what my father would want. He taught law and politics at Hanover University in North Carolina. I was still trying to impress him, to be worthy." And yet it hadn't been enough if Levi was putting the time-line together correctly. Marsh and Jefferson had still been estranged at the time of Jefferson's death.

The expression on Marsh's face changed, shifted to somber reflection as he stared into the fire. "Instead, it cost me the man I was going to marry. Patrick was smart, charming, dynamite in bed, and had the most amazing hair." A hint of a wistful smile drifted across his face but was gone the next second. "My moms loved him, I loved him, but that wasn't enough, not with me half a world away."

"I can't tell you how many relationships and marriages I saw crash and burn during deployments," Levi said. He'd seen it play out time and again on base and with family friends. Hell, Bella's marriage was almost a casualty of the same. "If my parents didn't love each other so damn much, they wouldn't have made it either, especially with Mom putting down roots and Dad deployed."

"That wasn't a life Patrick could accept, especially not with me hung up on the worst man in my life instead of the best." Marsh tapped his chest, right over his heart. "I wasn't emotionally available for him, and now that's my own curse."

"Your curse?" Levi asked, confused.

Until Marsh turned his dark eyes to him again and clarity struck like a lightning bolt, sizzling with Marsh's words. "Falling for emotionally unavailable men."

Oh.

TWENTY-ONE

LEVI SHOT out of his chair so fast Marsh had to rock back in his to avoid a collision. "I'll go get us a refill," Levi said, booking it to the kitchen—with only one glass—like his ass was on fire.

And his ass was fire.

And Marsh probably shouldn't have laid it all out there like that, but the past twenty-four hours had been excruciating… and wonderful.

He *liked* being Levi's husband. Liked holding his hand, liked being near him, liked watching Levi's mother sing her son's praises. For all Margaret's excitement over introducing the newest member of her family, it hadn't really been about Marsh. It had been about Levi. About her son, who was smart, devoted, and worked hard to give David the life he deserved. Her son who had found love and happiness again after having it so cruelly snatched away the first time.

Marsh was going to hate to have to disappoint her—and himself. Because after last night at Levi's parents' place and this evening at June's wedding, he was falling for his husband, harder and faster by the minute. Levi was all those things his mother had said and more. He was also tired, lonely, and stretched too thin. He was kind, and generous, and self-sacrificial. He was effortlessly sexy and aching to be taken. He needed more, and fuck it, Marsh wanted to give it to him. Regardless of their rules and regardless of how much it was going to fucking hurt when disappointment arrived. Until then, Marsh would wallow in the fiction they'd created long enough to give Levi what he needed.

He snatched his glass off the fire pit's ledge, flicked off the gas flame, and followed Levi inside.

Back to the door, Levi stood braced against the island, arms spread, knuckles white from his death grip around the edge. His torso rose and fell at a quickened clip, his efforts at deep breathing failing. The position, the motion, drew Marsh's attention to his broad shoulders and tapered back, to his trim waist, to his firm, round ass framed in slim-fitting suit pants.

Did he have any idea how sexy he was? And how had all those other people, besides Kristin, missed Levi's longing to set aside all that strength and let someone else drive? He could have been standing there in baggy pajamas and that thought alone would have turned Marsh on.

He stepped behind Levi and reached under one arm, sliding his glass onto the island. "You forgot this."

Levi didn't startle and didn't try to move away. His breath hitched once, then settled. Acceptance? Resignation? Desire getting the better of him too? "I needed a minute."

Marsh crowded closer. "Is that what you needed?" With the arm still under Levi's, he splayed a hand over toned abs and pressed Levi's back against his front, holding him firm. "Or is this?" Levi trembled in his arms, and Marsh nuzzled behind his ear, inhaling enticing freshness. "Ask for it," he rumbled, deep and with the hint of the demand he knew Levi needed.

"Marsh..." Levi didn't exactly relax in his arms, but he tipped his ass up, rubbing against Marsh as if he couldn't help himself. "If Brax and Sean were emotionally unavailable..."

"Smart. You caught that?" He skated his lips along Levi's skin, a trail from his ear to his collar.

Levi dropped his head onto Marsh's shoulder, giving him better access. "Impossible not to."

"This isn't about what I need." He nosed Levi's collar aside and licked a stripe across his tendon. A distraction while he slid his hand lower, palming Levi over his suit pants. Holding him firm there too. "It's about what you need."

Levi rocked into the touch, and his voice shook with restraint. "I need—"

Marsh curled his fingers over the ridge of Levi's erection and stroked. "Ask for it, Levi."

Levi's head lolled on his shoulder, his voice skating a plaintive edge. "I can't."

He eased his grip and softened his voice so as not to be an order. "Do you want me to stop?" he asked, needing an answer before he continued.

Levi shook his head.

"I need to hear you, Levi. Need you to consent."

"No."

Marsh's heart skipped.

"Don't stop."

Then galloped. He caressed Levi again. "You can't ask me to take you like this, hard and rough?" Used his other hand to palm Levi's rock-hard ass. "To shove my dick between these amazing cheeks?" Snaked it around to work loose Levi's belt and zipper. He dove his hand inside Levi's pants, inside his boxers and took the hard, heavy weight of Levi in his fist. "To pin you down to the bed and fuck you into the mattress?"

Levi groaned and tipped forward, catching himself with his hands on the island, thrusting back against Marsh's crotch, then forward to tunnel his dick into Marsh's fist in long sure strokes, slicking Marsh's grip with precome.

"Because I would." He gathered Levi's dress shirt with his other hand, yanking it up, putting his palm back on bare flesh, and stretched his body over Levi's, thrusting his own aching erection against the ass rutting against him. "But I wouldn't let you come. You'd be screwing the mattress while I screwed you, while I pumped into you and filled you up if you'd let me."

"I would," Levi gasped, and Marsh nearly exploded on the spot.

"You'd want me bare? All of this in you?" He notched his dick right against Levi's crack, teasing where he wanted to be. "I'm negative."

"So am I," Levi said on a groan Marsh felt against his chest, down to his dick, and in his hand around Levi's.

"It would feel so good," he said, sharing some of the mind-blowing fantasies unspooling in his head. "After I came inside your tight ass, I'd turn you over, lay you out, and watch my come leak out of you. Clean you up with my tongue, kiss the insides of your thighs, roll your balls around in my mouth." He kicked Levi's legs wider, dipped his hand lower, and fondled his balls. "Just like this."

Levi started to melt, legs shaking, thrusts becoming erratic. He turned his head toward Marsh, lips seeking, but Marsh dodged, nipped the tendon of his neck, and rubbed his scruff across it. "Work you over until your thighs were red from this beard, until you were out of your mind and begging me to let you come."

Levi gave up, head hanging forward. "I need to, Marsh, please."

Marsh hauled him off the island, back up against him, dick in his hand once more. His hold firm all over. "Only then would I take this thick, heavy cock in my mouth, all the way to the back of my throat." He stroked from the root to the tip with a twist. "And you'd feel me tell you to *come*."

Levi jerked in his arms, erupting onto his stomach, the island, and Marsh's fist. "Fuck."

Marsh wasn't through with him yet, though. Wasn't through with the fantasy he was going to go upstairs and jerk off to as soon as they were done. "I'd swallow all this come down." He spread his messy hand, Levi's release, all over Levi's belly, evidence of the need he'd rendered. "Then I'd crawl up your beautiful body." He rutted his own against it and ran his lips along Levi's jaw to the underside of his chin. Close to where Levi wanted it, where Marsh fucking wanted it desperately, but where they couldn't go without disappointment crashing the release they'd both needed. "I'd kiss you so you could taste us, then, if I was hard again, which at my age is a big *if*, I'd straddle you, jerk myself off, and come all over you."

Levi's second jolt was a sexy, pleasant surprise, and the last of Levi's tension seeped away, his body melting fully into Marsh's. Marsh wrapped both arms around him, heedless of the mess, too caught up in the warmth and intimacy of the moment. As Levi drifted, he nuzzled his nape, dropping light kisses there until he shuffled them to the other side of the island, to where he could hold Levi while filling a glass of water. He set it on the island in front of Levi, waiting for him to drain it and get his legs back under him. When he was sure Levi could stand on his own, he loosened his hold and lightly grasped Levi's chin, drawing his blown-wide gaze around to him. "All you have to do is ask, Levi. Ask for what you need, and I'll give it to you."

He released Levi's chin and moved to go, but Levi's steel grip around his wrist halted him in his tracks. "What about you?"

Marsh lifted his wrist, Levi's hand with it, and kissed his knuckles. "Not tonight. Tonight was for you. What *you* needed." He adjusted his grip, his hand directing Levi's over the erection straining behind his zipper. "But if you hear some grunts from the guest bathroom"—he thrust against Levi's palm, then let his hand go and stepped away —"rest assured, baby, you gave me what I needed too."

TWENTY-TWO

IF LEVI HEARD ANY GRUNTS, it was all of two. Marsh was so turned on by Levi moaning and writhing— coming apart—in his arms that it was a miracle he made it upstairs to the guest bathroom without coming in his pants. He shut the door behind him, dropped his slacks, peeled off his precome-soaked boxers, and wrenched on the hot water. Stepping under the spray, he closed his eyes, fisted his erection, and imagined Levi facedown on the bed, his glorious ass in the air, his hole filled by Marsh's bare cock. Two twisting jerks of his hand later, Marsh coated the shower wall.

He stayed under the spray until the water began to cool, hoping it would nudge his libido the same direction. He felt marginally less like a live wire when he lay down in bed and shut his eyes, but it wasn't long before his brain began feeding him images of a debauched Levi.

Come-covered and spread out under him in bed.

Laid out on the kitchen island, back arched and cock straining for Marsh's mouth.

Standing naked in front of the primary bedroom's giant windows, arms and legs spread, his erect cock pressed against the glass, streaking it with precome, while Marsh tongue-fucked his hole.

Image after image that Marsh had no business conjuring up about his husband. Marsh had known keeping this arrangement professional would be a long shot—he'd been attracted to Levi from the word go—but the crushing lust, the fact that he was exactly the sort of bottom Marsh craved... He knew better. He'd seen the porn in Levi's supposedly deleted browser history, but he'd initially made the same assumptions others had about Levi. That maybe submission wasn't really what he wanted. But downstairs tonight proved exactly how much Levi wanted it.

Needed it.

And proved exactly how far—how unprofessional—Marsh was willing to go to make sure Levi had what he needed.

Maybe they could make it work for the duration of the mission. Something casual.

Brax and Sean laughed in his head.

With good reason. Marsh didn't know how to do casual. He knew how to fall, hard and fast. The end. And a love-sick cowboy was the last thing Levi needed, not with every-thing else he had to juggle—work, David, his family. No, he needed Marsh to pull it together, to help him solve his case so he could get on with the life he was supposed to be putting back together.

One that did not include Marsh.

But if Levi asked...

Marsh shoved a hand inside his shorts and fisted his cock. Stroked it a couple times, then heaved a heavy sigh when semierect was the best he got. Like he'd told Levi, whether he'd get hard a second time was a dicey proposition at forty-six. No shame, just biology. Maybe if he had the real thing in his bed instead of the porn reel in his head... He shook off the thought; that wasn't happening tonight. Which left only one thing to do. The same thing he'd done all those nights in the army when he'd been too turned on to think straight and had nowhere to stick his dick. He hauled his ass out of bed, booted up his computer, and got to work.

And stayed at it until the morning sun began to peek into the east-facing window beside his desk. He removed his glasses, rubbed his tired eyes, and dreamed about the coffee that was in his near future. But first, he needed to be sure. He slid the frames back on and reviewed the documents on the dual monitors. It wasn't rock solid, but it was another lead. One that might give them enough info to locate and disrupt the next transfer scheduled for Friday. He grabbed his phone off the charger and shot off a text to Matt. **Apologies for the early hour and on a Sunday. May have something. Meet us at the house?**

Marsh hadn't been to the office that many days, but on each one of them, Matt had been there before him and Levi. Early riser, Marsh guessed. Guessed right. **I can be there in an hour**, came the text back.

Perfect.

Marsh had another motive, of course. By inviting Matt over, by jumping into case work first thing, it would spare Levi feeling or acting awkward about last night. With company and work top of mind, he and Levi could get back to being professional. Easier said than done. Too few minutes later, there was a knock on the door, sooner than expected, and Marsh emerged from his office... to run right into a freshly showered Levi at the top of the stairs. Barefoot, Levi was dressed in cargo shorts and a red tee, and as water dripped from the ends of his damp hair, Marsh followed a droplet that dipped into the divot at the bottom of his neck and disappeared under his collar, traveling unseen over the toned chest and abs Marsh had had his hands all over last night.

"Marsh, you okay?"

His gaze shot up, and he chuckled at Levi's raised brow. "Yeah, sorry." He removed his glasses again and did a whole face swipe this time. "Long night."

"You don't say."

Marsh expected regret, maybe anger, definitely awkwardness, but when he opened his eyes, Levi's crooked smile was charmingly amused.

"Working," Marsh said, needing that smile gone before he grabbed Levi by the waist, shoved his shirt up, and found out exactly where that droplet had gone.

"Oh."

He hated how fast Levi's smile fell. "To keep my mind off the other things I'd rather be doing."

Heat lit Levi's cheeks, and Marsh was two seconds away from giving them the kiss they both wanted when another knock sounded against the door.

"I asked Matt to swing by. Something I worked up last night I wanted to show you both." He raked a hand through his hair and gave it a tug, still feeling half in a daze. "Give me ten to wash up. He got here faster than I thought he would."

"Or you lost track of time."

"Probably. Hacker problem."

Levi skirted past him and started down the stairs. "I'll get your coffee going."

Marsh took a few seconds to breathe in Levi's lingering citrusy scent before it became tinged with peppermint, then hustled to shower and change himself. He was downstairs in seven and found Matt leaned over the chess set on the breakfast table, Marsh and David's game from yesterday not yet finished.

"He's got you here," Matt said, gesturing to David's pawn that was two squares from checking his king.

"Except it's my move next, and he's forgotten about my wing pawn here."

"Think David's realized it yet?" Levi said, handing Marsh a double espresso.

"Ooh," Matt said, eyeing the double shot. "Someone didn't sleep."

"Family wedding," Levi said, sparing him.

"Say no more," Matt said with a flitting hand. "Fairly certain it was a family wedding that made my little brother run away." Before Marsh could follow up on that revealing bit of the other agent's past, Matt focused them on the present. "You texted that you had something?"

"Easier if I show you." Marsh downed the espresso, set his glass in the sink, and led Levi and Matt upstairs to the office.

"Did we find out who's number that was on Frederick's phone? George Washington?"

"I'll get to that," Marsh said. He claimed his chair and began maximizing windows. When he had everything ready, he turned half-around so he could see Levi and Matt and they could see his screen. "Something Levi and I talked about last night got me thinking."

Matt's brow shot up so fast Marsh thought it might fly away. When both Marsh and Levi laughed, the other brow lifted to match, Matt glancing back and forth between them. "I thought this was fake."

"We do both currently live in this house"—Marsh twirled a finger in the air, gesturing around them—"and conversate."

"Conversate... Right..."

All that intel on Agent Kim being a top-notch investigator wasn't wrong. Said investigator also made the smart play and decided not to press his suspects—Marsh and Levi —further about personal details, turning instead to the professional, thank fuck. "What'd you find, Agent Marshall?"

"When we talked about the desert," Marsh said, angled toward Levi, "about how I kept coming back to it, it made me think about something in your case."

"Our case?" Matt said.

"Yes, the one with the traffickers—Orchard—here, stateside. Why do they keep coming back to San Diego? Especially when they know the local FBI field office is actively investigating?"

"Ports, rail, major interstates, proximity to Mexico," Matt rattled off.

But Levi was the one following Marsh's train of thought, the two of them in sync. "It's home. Even if it's EC in Vienna holding the purse strings, we always figured there had to be someone local involved."

"Frederick and Johnny only moved here within the past year," Marsh said as he displayed their change of address forms from the USPS. "But do you know who's born and raised in San Diego?"

"Amanda Hudson?" Matt ventured.

"Correct." Marsh pulled up the driver's license of the third person in the trio. "And do you know where Amanda Hudson volunteers her time?" He maximized the web browser with the site he had open. "The Sixth Avenue Shelter."

"I know that one!" Matt said. "I volunteer at the soup kitchen when I can. Heavy immigrant population."

"Ripe for the picking." Marsh opened a larger window where he had eight photos assembled, each next to a surveillance still from the shelter. "These photos correspond to missing persons over the past twelve months. All of them stayed at least one night at that shelter."

Matt stepped closer and stared at the screen. "None of these names are familiar. None of them came up in the missing persons reports."

"Because all these women overstayed their visas. Their absences weren't—couldn't be—reported officially without involving immigration. I found their information through unofficial forums. Immigrant communities always find a way."

"They do," Matt echoed.

"Eight women," Marsh said. "All between the ages of eighteen and twenty-five, all on expiring visas."

Levi put it all together. "It's not only Frederick we need to be pressuring. It's Amanda."

Marsh nodded. "Even more so when we get back to Agent Kim's initial question."

"Who's George Washington?" Matt asked again.

This time, Marsh gave him the answer. "Greg Hudson, Amanda's father, and the Assistant Director of the Sixth Avenue Shelter."

TWENTY-THREE

LEVI WAS LEANED over his desk next to Marsh, examining funds flow information Frederick had coughed up in the name of cooperation and leniency, when Matt knocked on the open door and stuck his head inside.

"Let's go," he said. "Kwan's back and has fifteen before her next meeting."

He moved on without waiting for them to follow. "That's good luck," Levi said as they gathered everything back into folders. When they'd looked at her calendar yesterday for a spot today, she was scheduled to be out of the office in the morning and booked solid the rest of the afternoon. Levi was prepared to have to write everything up, had asked Marsh to go over it all again one more time so he didn't get any of the details wrong, but he would much rather present their case to her live with Marsh's direct input.

"The mission," Marsh said. "That's what Kwan is all about, and this is a critical one for her. She won't let it go sideways again." He tucked one folder under his arm and held out the rest to him. "Sell it."

Levi's stomach sank; he was really starting to hate those words. Hated the implication of those files midhandoff between them even more. "You're not coming?"

"This is your case. You should be the one to bring it home."

Levi accepted the files, mostly to cover the worry that swirled in his gut. Worry that Marsh was pulling away, that the distance that was always supposed to stay between them, that they'd recklessly chipped away at until it had all but vanished Saturday night, was back and on its way to being as wide and deep as the canyon behind his house. Worry that he was never going to get the kiss that had eluded him Saturday, that had run roughshod over his imagination since. More than his own reckless desire, though, was pride for what his team had pulled together, including Marsh's invaluable contributions. "But *you* delivered us this lead. *You* identified the connections."

"And while you pitch our theory to Kwan, I'm going to go upstairs, knock out this matter for SAC Bell, then get back to work on our friend Stefan."

Levi didn't have a response. Marsh was in the right on all counts, but this felt all wrong.

Until Marsh stepped closer and lightly cupped his elbow. "Hey," he rumbled in the quiet comforting tone that had earnestly asked for his consent Saturday night. "You know what you need to do. I just got you there faster." He firmed his grip. "This is the part you're good at. I've seen it."

Levi soaked up the reassurance, professionally and personally, steadying his insides and straightening his back, bringing him almost eye level with Marsh, whose slow satisfied grin nearly had Levi grabbing for his shirt.

"Go get the authorization to proceed, put the pressure on Greg and Amanda, and let's find out when and where this next transfer is going to happen. Then I'll be ready to deal with Stefan. Sound like a plan?"

Levi nodded. "Sounds like a plan."

Marsh's hand on the small of his back as they left the office was a bonus, a step back from the canyon's edge. They parted at the break in the bullpen for the elevator lobby, Marsh heading up, Levi the rest of the way across the bullpen to where Matt waited outside the ASAC's office.

"He's not coming with?" Matt asked.

"He's following the Stefan lead for us, which I don't think we should tell Kwan about without him. It's not pertinent to our op." Stefan and EC were Marsh's case, phase two of the bigger picture if they accomplished what they needed to on phase one. Better to focus Kwan's attention on the first mission, the relatively easier one to win.

"Agreed," Matt said.

"I also don't want to get him or Kwan in hot water with the SAC since Marsh is supposed to be working on a case for him."

"Good, let him keep Bell distracted."

"What's that supposed to mean?"

"Means I'd rather deal with Kwan"—he rapped his knuckles against the door—"than that asshole any day of the week."

"Come in," the ASAC called from inside, and Matt pushed the door open before Levi could reply. Kwan stood behind her desk, waiting for them with her hands on her hips. "Agents," she said, "I understand there are more developments."

"We've got a likely date for the next transfer," Levi said, "and a lead on the location with a possible way to narrow that down."

She waved them over to the round table in the corner of her office. "Show me what you've got."

They filled her in on the details and the picture they'd put together—Frederick laundering for Orchard, the date the next payment was set to go out, the missing women at the shelter, the Hudsons' ties to the shelter and to Orchard —and finally their proposed next steps—question Amanda after her arraignment before she makes bail, and her father if they needed to, and try and get a firmer location on which Withers rail facility would be used for the exchange with Frederick in the wings to cut off the funds flow if they needed to take more drastic action.

Kwan spent several minutes looking over the evidence and asking the follow-up questions they'd expected and were prepared to answer. Eventually, she stood back, arms crossed, and Levi counted to five before he opened his mouth to lobby harder.

She held up a hand. "No need, Agent Bishop. You get me a location on that exchange, and I'll authorize the op."

"We're on it," Matt said as Levi gathered the files together.

They were almost out the door when her earlier frown cracked the opposite direction. "Nice work, you three."

♙♙♗♙♙♙♙♕♙♙

COURTROOM   DELAYS   PUSHED   Amanda's arraignment to early afternoon. While they couldn't nail her on embezzlement, there was more than enough evidence to hold and arraign her for felony assault on a federal officer. Since they knew where she was for the next few hours, Matt suggested they work another angle in the meantime. Which was how Levi ended up at the Sixth Avenue Shelter, ladling soup next to Matt, who was gently probing the cook, JoJo, for information.

"How's everyone been doing lately?"

"Good," she replied from a good half foot over Matt's and Levi's heads. She handed a bowl to a woman in her midforties, if Levi had to guess, older for the general age of folks they'd served so far. "Here you go, Dana." JoJo gave her a kind smile that was hospitality industry practiced. Levi remembered it well.

Matt picked up on the same. "You're not so sure," he said once there was a break in the line.

JoJo pushed a dyed blue braid back under her hairnet. "We've lost a couple regulars."

"Lost?"

"AWOL." Judging by the faded trident tattoo on JoJo's left shoulder that Levi had glimpsed before she'd slipped on her chef's coat, Levi guessed navy, a former SEAL.

"Good way, maybe?"

"Unlikely."

"You've checked hospitals?" Levi asked.

She nodded. "Asked around, but it's hard when no one uses their real name."

"We can try to look," Matt offered.

JoJo withdrew a scratch pad and pen from the pocket of her chef's coat and jotted down their names and descriptions. Levi thought one might be a match from Marsh's list, but the other was new.

"Did you bring it up with the director or assistant director?" Matt asked.

"Director helped me look. As for the assistant director…" She pulled a face that reminded Levi of the first time three-year-old David had picked up a fallen lemon from the tree in their yard and bit into it. "He's a glorified penny pincher." Add anger to sour, her dark cheeks reddening. "Not a social worker."

Matt clasped her muscled arm. "Thank God for you, JoJo."

They got back to ladling soup until service was over, JoJo offering them both a bowl before heading into the kitchen. Matt claimed one of the open tables, and Levi noticed that those who came and went in the mess hall gave them a wide berth. "Folks here know you're law enforcement?" he surmised.

Matt nodded. "I've been volunteering since I arrived here, and there've been no ICE incidents, but still, they keep their distance."

Levi tasted a spoonful of soup and immediately went back for several more. The minestrone was nothing like his mother's recipe, but it was amazing. Lighter on the tomato, heavier on the vegetables, the flavor deep yet fresh. "This is really good."

"No shit," Matt said around a mouthful. "JoJo's a Michelin-starred chef. Also a washed-out SEAL that became homeless because she wanted to live as her true self. She found herself and her talent working the shelter soup kitchen where she lived for a while in LA. I knew her through my brother even before I moved here. Hell, she's the one who talked up San Diego when I was considering the assignment. Left out the bit about the planes, though."

Levi chuckled and used the lighter mood to follow up on another question that had nagged him. "So you're in touch with your brother again?"

Matt's expression, the locked-down one he reserved for interrogations, did not match his words. "We're one of the lucky families."

The older woman from earlier slid onto the bench beside Matt. "I heard you asking JoJo about the missing women. You think you can help find them?"

"We're gonna try," Matt said. "Dana, right?"

"They're not the first," Dana replied.

Levi checked with Matt, who nodded, before he revealed several of the other names from Marsh's list.

"Don't know them," Dana said. "Haven't been here long. But I heard Claire"—one of the women on JoJo's list—"talking with Keira"—a new name—"a few days ago. Said Amanda, the assistant director's daughter who volunteers here, had an opportunity for them in Missouri. A job, money enough to buy a house, papers. Asked her to 'keep it quiet,' but Keira doesn't know the meaning of the word."

"She say anything else?" Matt said.

"Asked if I wanted to go too."

"And you said no?"

"My kid's here." She looked both proud and sad. "She doesn't know me, but I gotta make sure the people who adopted her do her right, you know?"

Matt edged a hand her direction, waited, and when she didn't flinch, covered hers with his. Waited another minute before speaking again. "Did they say when or where?"

"Don't have a where, but I do gotta when. Thursday."

Made sense. A day before the payment was set to deposit.

"This is helpful," Levi said. "Thank you."

"Claire's a good kid. Keira too, even if she does run her mouth too much. They're both young enough for a second chance."

Matt squeezed her hand. "We're never too old for second chances." Levi didn't think Matt was only talking about Dana.

TWENTY-FOUR

LEVI AND MATT stood as the interrogation room door opened, Amanda's attorney ushering her client in. "You've got until my client makes bail," Gail MacDonald said.

Gail was one of the toughest defense attorneys in town... and one of the most respected, even by law enforcement. She didn't take the easy way out, didn't purposefully try to make LEOs' lives difficult just to get her high-paying clients off. She made Levi and his colleagues work to be better, be the best, same as she was.

She also didn't beat around the bush. She'd let them know they had five, ten minutes tops, to question Amanda. Levi didn't mince words. "Would that be your father posting bail?"

Matt didn't waste time either. "Did he get the money from the traffickers you're sending victims? From Orchard Investments?"

"Don't answer that," Gail said from her chair beside Amanda.

From the folder on the table between them, Levi withdrew the photo stills of the ten missing women. "Ten victims that we know of have gone missing, all with connections to the Sixth Avenue Shelter, all who overstayed their visas and remain here without a visa or green card. No one's officially reported them missing."

"If they're not reported missing," Gail said, "you have no case."

He pushed forward the photo of Keira that Marsh had captured for them. "Except one of them talked."

Amanda went stiff in her chair.

"Claire, here"—Matt pushed Claire's photo out of the lineup, next to Keira's—"convinced Keira to come with her, and then Keira tried to convince someone else at the shelter. They were escaping to Missouri, our source said, based on the promise of a job and money enough to buy a house. Leaving on Thursday."

"Would you know anything about that?" Matt said.

Still no response, though Amanda was pressing her lips together as if fighting to stay quiet.

Levi pushed some more. "See, we could trace the funds Johnny and Frederick were laundering, Johnny for himself, Frederick for himself and Orchard, but we could never trace any to you."

"Get to the point, agents," Gail said.

"It was never you that got paid, was it?" Levi said. "It wasn't your money that needed laundering."

"Did Johnny find out?" Matt pressed. "Is that why you introduced him to Frederick, who was laundering money for your dad?"

Amanda couldn't keep a lid on it any longer, her dark eyes glittering with fury, her voice shaking with it when she spoke again. "That asshole tried to blackmail me. Me!"

Gail put a hand on her forearm, aiming to calm. "Amanda."

"No! I have more important things to do than deal with some idiot who couldn't get his dick up who is now trying to salvage his fragile manhood by lording this over me."

"More important things like delivering women for Orchard to Stefan Sanders," Levi said.

Amanda smacked the metal table. "Yes!"

The door behind them banged open, and a middle-aged man with brown hair and deep lines at the corners of his eyes and mouth stepped inside. "That's enough, Amanda. Let's go. We're done here." He yanked her up by the arm, then turned a pointed finger on Gail. "And you're fired."

He hauled Amanda out of the room, leaving Levi, Matt, and Gail in a daze. The latter found her words first. "If I can get her to talk, can we cut a deal?"

"I'll see what I can do," Levi said. "But didn't Greg just fire you?"

Gail's killer smile made Levi fear for Greg's balls. "The engagement letter says I represent Amanda and only Amanda on this matter. She's an adult. Only she can fire me, not her father. It's my ethical obligation to get her the best deal. And my moral one to get you that information."

"You've still got my number?" Matt said.

"I do. And you have mine." Her killer smile turned flirtatious, and Levi suspected she'd had Matt's balls too but in the good way.

"We have until Thursday," Matt said.

"I'll see what *I* can do."

Levi sincerely hoped her departing wink wasn't the only thing she threw their way.

♟♙♟♟♟♟♟♙♟♟

WHILE LEVI and Matt continued to run down leads on Orchard Investments, the Sixth Avenue Shelter, and the Hudsons, Marsh distracted himself from the unsettled feeling of being on the outside—despite being the one that put himself there, for good reasons—by working Bell's identity theft case.

A rash of bank transfers had been reported to the FBI, all of them while the victims were on vacation, all the victims having traveled to said vacations on the same airline, albeit to different locations. A few phone calls and it became clear the initial theft of identity was related to the credit card applications each of the victims had filled out on the plane. From there, things got trickier... and twistier. He'd had to navigate between banks and brokerage firms who weren't supposed to authorize transfers between accounts without multiple checks—what good was two-factor authentication if a bank didn't follow its own rules—but because the thieves had their victims' almighty social security numbers and enough other identifying information, the damage was done. Marsh had eventually identified the IP addresses of the persons who'd provided the passengers' information and of the person who'd initiated the transfers to fake accounts set up in the victims' names but controlled by the thieves. Money that, in at least one case, had already been cashed out. He'd initiated warrants for each of the IP addresses and, while those processed, followed the IP addresses to wherever they led.

To forged driver's licenses. Real names and information but with pictures that did not match those of the victims.

Marsh had encrypted confirmations of the orders coming in and going out. None of the licenses he tracked had been confiscated by law enforcement yet—top-notch forgeries assisted by digital identity theft.

All tracing back to the same IP address.

Five of them matching shelter women he'd ID'd in Levi's case.

"Hey, Farmer, can I get your eyes on something?"

The only other cyber agent who'd stayed to work through lunch looked up, his brows racing for the hairline of his short-clipped hair. "Me?"

"Yeah, you." Marsh waved him over. "You're a cyber agent, aren't you?"

"I am."

"Well, I need a cyber agent consult."

"But you're—" The younger Black man rose and crossed the cyber bullpen to the desk beside Marsh's borrowed one. If his buzz cut hadn't given it away, his efficient steps and straight-backed bearing did.

"Which branch?" Marsh asked.

"Army, 101st Airborne."

"No shit? Screaming Eagles?"

"Until I broke every bone in my right leg on a jump." He hitched up his right pant leg, showing off his prosthetic.

Marsh whistled appreciatively. "Nice."

"Thanks, yeah, so..." He lowered his pant leg and his chin. "I was with the 101st but got my degree in crypto. Would probably still be in the army if I'd gone into cyber warfare. Liked jumping out of planes more. My mama will never forgive me." He shrugged. "But I hung around cyber too. Helped when I could. Respectfully, sir, you're a fucking legend."

The compliment did Marsh's soul good, but his body had other ideas. "A legend with old, tired eyes and a headache." He tilted his head toward his monitors, and Farmer wheeled closer. "I'm looking into these forged IDs." He indicated the screen on the left. "Which trace back to the same IP address linked to this identity theft case." Indicated the right screen. "You see anything I did wrong? Any other direction it could go?"

Farmer spent several minutes clicking through windows, reviewing Marsh's work, asking follow-up questions, and it was a delight to converse with someone on that level again, reminded him of what it used to be like with Holt by his side at Camp Casey. Agent Farmer's ultimate conclusion—"This is solid work"—was the one Marsh both wanted and was afraid of.

He'd not misstepped, but now he was left sitting on his hands, waiting for those warrants to come through.

"Thank you, Agent Farmer." He began closing windows until Farmer pointed at the screen, finger hovering just above it over the second to last ID.

"Wait! She looks familiar. Did you run her through facial recognition?"

"I did. No match." The white woman pictured on the Washington state driver's license appeared to be in her midtwenties, dark hair and blue eyes, no identifying marks or features visible from her headshot.

Farmer started for the keyboard, then caught himself, hands up, palms out. "Sorry, that was rude," he said. "It's just—"

"A force of habit?" Marsh knew it well as both a hacker and investigator. When he saw a lead he wanted to chase, it was like his fingers and the keys were magnets drawn to each other.

"A rude one, but yes. May I?"

"By all means." Marsh scooted over giving Farmer access to the keyboard.

He opened a terminal window, then a search program he accessed on a private server. "Little something I designed. It's a broader search than official channels. Because of—"

"The immigrant population here." Made sense. Hadn't Marsh done the same—*Wait*. Foreboding settled heavy on Marsh's shoulders. "Could this be connected?" He was referring to his and Levi's cases, but Farmer took the utterance more broadly.

"Worth a look," he said. Turned out he was right. It took his custom search less than a minute to turn up a news story about a prostitution sting from last winter. The woman in the license photo was the same one being questioned by an officer in the background of the newscaster's breaking news segment on the sting. "The search isn't turning up a positive ID on her, though."

"Can you add another source parameter?" Marsh said. "Like traffic and ATM cams?"

"If you've got a location."

Marsh provided the Sixth Avenue Shelter address, Farmer keyed it in, set a two-block radius, and facial recognition began whirring again. What was it Marsh had said—tired eyes? Tired brain too it seemed. He hadn't thought to run it against his prior searches, not that he had access to his personal computer and the info there. He trusted Farmer had taken all precautions, that the crypto specialist in him would've covered his tracks.

Facial recognition pinged. "That's her," Farmer said. "Walking into the shelter three days ago."

Make that eleven potential victims. Though this one was not a past victim. She was likely in the current batch of trafficking victims, hence the ID. What about the others? "Can you run these others through your program?" he said to Farmer as he stood. "See if any of the rest of them are connected to the shelter?"

"You got it."

Marsh grabbed two folders and the ID printouts from the printer and was halfway to the door, on his way to the elevators and Levi, when the phone in his pocket vibrated. He opened the email, seeing the warrant approvals for the IP addresses.

Bingo!

TWENTY-FIVE

FUCK BINGO. Marsh did not like the prize he'd won. *At all.*

He knocked on the war room door, and all four heads inside—Levi's, Matt's, Alyssa's, and Will's—swiveled his direction.

Marsh held up two file folders. "Have something you might want to see."

Levi straightened from where he stood leaning over one end of the oval table. "On Stefan?"

"Haven't gotten that far yet." He entered the conference room and immediately noticed the whiteboard covered in notes and photos now had a solid line drawn between Amanda and Stefan. "But it looks like you have. You confirmed they're working together?"

"She let that slip when we questioned her." Levi strolled around the table to stand next to him in front of the board, and that nagging unsettled feeling tugging at Marsh's insides eased. "Johnny found out and was blackmailing her."

"To skim some money for himself?"

"Idiot out for a buck," Matt said. "Stuck his nose in the wrong mess."

"The *way* wrong mess," Alyssa added from behind them. Marsh rotated away from the board, the same direction as Levi, and the lingering citrus and peppermint scent settled Marsh further. When Levi's elbow brushed against his, he didn't step away. And neither did Levi.

"As we suspected," Matt said, "Amanda identifies the victims at the shelter, lures them to a meeting point, then coordinates delivery at a transfer point with Stefan. Her attorney is working to get us a more precise location on the Thursday meet-up."

"Thursday?"

"From a source at the shelter," Levi said.

"This might help." Marsh dropped one of the folders onto the table. "More victims for your board. The top one, Maria, is probably caught up in this Thursday's transport."

Will opened the folder and pulled the top photo closer to where he, Matt, and Alyssa stood by the table. "How'd you ID her?"

"I was asked to look into an identity theft case, which led me to forged licenses, one for Maria among them. Ran her against facial recognition and picked her up entering the shelter three days ago." He dropped the second folder on the table. "Dug some more, and I found fake IDs for at least five other women on your board, plus two others who were new to me."

Matt practically lunged for the rest of the photos, shuffling through them until he pulled out the two unknowns. "Fuck, these have gotta be Claire and Keira." He snapped a picture with his phone. "I'm sending to JoJo to confirm."

"Our source at the shelter overheard them talking," Levi explained. "That's how we found out about Thursday."

"JoJo says that's them," Matt chimed in.

"Who's the forger?" Alyssa asked.

Marsh eyed her and Will. "You two mind giving us the room?"

"Look," Will said, straightening, "we're on this team too."

Marsh raised a hand. "And I'm sure Levi and Matt will loop you in as they see fit, including on the operation itself..."

"We're already planning for that," Levi said, thankfully following his lead. "There are office politics involved here, higher up, because of us"—he gestured between him and Marsh—"being married."

Alyssa, hand to Will's shoulder, steered him toward the door. "You're new here. Trust me, if they're giving us an out on this, we should take it. 'Office politics' is code for bullshit, and we've got better things to do."

Marsh mouthed a "Thank you" to her as he closed the door behind them.

"I hope I wasn't lying just now," Levi said to him.

"You weren't." He shoved his hands in his pockets and leaned back against the door. "Blaine Anthony."

"What about him?" Levi said.

"He's the son of Representative Anthony, right?" Matt said. "Right-wing prick with a hard-on for the presidency?"

"That's the one," Levi said with a nod. "Fancies himself Reagan 2.0. He's also the SAC's tennis partner."

And fucking bingo again. Marsh idly contemplated federal action to ban the game before sharing his winnings with Matt and Levi. "Blaine's the forger."

Levi's slack-jawed, "Wait, what?" collided with Matt's disbelieving, "Repeat that."

"Blaine Anthony is the person who forged those IDs, including the ones for Maria, Claire, and Keira." He went ahead and gave them all the bad news. Shared the pain he wasn't willing to inflict on Alyssa and Will for their own safety. "And I was explicitly asked by SAC Bell not to implicate Anthony's son in the identity theft case."

Matt gestured wildly toward the pictures scattered across the table. "But he's directly implicated."

"That's not our problem this week," Levi said grudgingly, his voice and frame vibrating with anger. So much so Marsh pushed off the wall to stand beside him, a hand on his lower back. His voice was a modicum steadier when he spoke again. "How do we use this information to rescue those women?"

"Representative Anthony sits on the committee that controls grant funding for shelters," Marsh said. "Including the Sixth Avenue Shelter."

"That's his leverage over the Hudsons," Matt said.

"Feed it to Gail," Levi said. "Threaten a broader investigation if they don't give us the Thursday details."

"Better leverage," Matt said with a nod as he pulled out his phone.

"But don't mention Anthony by name," Marsh said. "We just want to spook them, not set off so many alarm bells the op doesn't happen or moves somewhere we don't have eyes on."

"And tell Gail to tread carefully," Levi added.

"Got it." Phone in hand, Matt pivoted toward the other end of the conference room.

Marsh took Levi by the elbow and led him the opposite

direction. "If we do miss them here, I might have a lead on where the next transfer point is supposed to be."

"Somewhere between here and Missouri," Levi said, not stepping away when Marsh released his arm. "Keira told our source that was the destination."

Marsh withdrew his phone and opened the email and attached property listing that had arrived on his way down the stairs. He handed the device to Levi. "This random Orchard purchase of an industrial building outside Amarillo makes sense then."

Levi scrolled through the listing, thumb slowing over the screen. "No other real estate or investments in the area?"

"None, and it doesn't make sense with the rest of their portfolio, which is mostly Class A office space."

Levi handed the phone back. "This is where Stefan will be."

"Likely."

"Do we intercept there or here? Because if we intercept here, Stefan will bolt."

Marsh didn't hesitate with his answer. He'd known it even after he'd found the property in Texas. "If you get a location out of Amanda, intercept here in San Diego and move on Orchard."

"But your case—"

"No," Marsh said with a sharp shake of his head. "Your case is the one that matters more right now. Rescuing these women"—he jutted his chin at the photos on the table— "matters the most. I don't want to risk losing them again, we rescue them now, *here*, if we have that opportunity. And we stop Orchard from funding more operations like it."

Levi opened his mouth as if to say something, then

closed it as his brows snapped together. Then rose as his eyes grew wide. "It could've been Anthony that cratered our earlier operation."

"Could've been me too."

This time it was Levi who gave a sharp shake of his head. "I've watched you work these past few weeks. You're good at what you do. The best I've seen. I don't believe you screwed up."

Marsh lowered his chin, momentarily taken aback by the earnest faith in Levi's eyes. Faith in him. Levi's hand on his chest had him looking up. Would've had him leaning in if not for Matt at the other end of the room. Marsh settled for covering Levi's hand with his and forcing out a gruff "Thank you" around the surprising lump in his throat.

"We'll alert the Dallas field office. They've got jurisdiction over Amarillo," Levi said. "See if we can catch Stefan before he runs. I'm sorry—"

"Don't be," Marsh said with a squeeze of his hand. "This was always the plan. Disrupt their operation—turn off the supply of trafficking victims, infiltrate their funds flow—we lock Orchard down, we save those women, and then we force Eder to make other moves."

"And Gail is going to help us," Matt said. "She's meeting with Amanda again tonight."

"We need to work up a rough operational game plan for Kwan," Marsh said. "She'll expect that. Two fronts, the meet-up and Orchard."

"See if we can get on the ASAC's calendar for tomorrow morning," Levi said to Matt then swung his gaze to Marsh. "For all three of us," he said, voice brooking no argument.

If Levi kept looking at him like that, Marsh would never

argue with him about anything again... except maybe that whole leaf water thing.

TWENTY-SIX

"ALL THREE OF YOU THIS TIME?" Kwan said from across the table in her office.

Marsh expected Levi to come to his defense, but it was Matt who got there first. "Marsh was instrumental in getting us this far. He deserves to be here."

Kwan's assessing glare swung to him. "What about your identity theft case for SAC Bell?"

"I've made progress," he hedged.

Which she didn't buy. She knew him well enough to know that wasn't the whole story. Trusted him enough to let it go in this instance. She shifted her attention to Levi. "And how far are you?"

"We've got a location for both the first and second exchanges this time."

"Start with the backstop," Kwan said.

"Amarillo," Marsh replied as he handed her the Texas property listing. "Orchard Investments, the group behind the traffickers here, just bought an industrial property there."

"Will and Alyssa are already on the phone with the Dallas field office," Levi informed the ASAC. "Amarillo makes sense. It's a midpoint rail or car stop on the way to Missouri from Escondido."

"The first transfer point," Kwan correctly deduced.

"A rail yard there, according to Amanda, owned by Withers Transport. She gave each of the women—five this time, three we've identified—the address and a time to meet in the parking lot there. Said a van would pick them up and take them to a private airstrip and on to Missouri."

"But that's not what's going to happen."

"No, it's not," Matt said. "The traffickers will either have the usual under-the-radar-size moving truck there to pick them up, or they'll put them on a rail car. Rail yard gives them both options."

"Proximity to civilians?" Kwan asked. "If I recall, the rail lines in Escondido are mostly in commercial areas."

Levi spread the satellite photos he'd had blown up across the table. "Correct, but they're not doing this exchange in the dead of night. Amanda told them to meet at the pickup location at four."

"Cargo vessel that time of day?"

Levi nodded. "The last one until the next Monday."

"Why's that?"

Marsh pointed out the biggest problem on the map, two streets over from the commercial rail yard. "Because the local commuter transit center gets weekend priority."

"Rush hour is rush hour, no matter the weekday. Fuck." Kwan spun on her heel and paced the short distance between her desk and the table. "And there's no other intercept point before Amarillo?"

"Not that we know of," Marsh said. "We could put a tail on them here, pull them over on the freeway, but—"

Kwan didn't need him to finish; they'd been through enough tactical scenarios together to know the outcomes. "They could shake the tail. They could cause even more damage on the freeway. They could be traveling by rail, in which case, it's a total crapshoot. And who knows what would happen to those women by the time we intercepted." She returned to the table and traced the triangular area of the rail yard with her finger. "All right, show me how you propose to do this and keep it within that boundary?"

They walked her through the quick and dirty plan the team had put together. Let things appear as normal in the streets immediately around the rail yard, increased presence the next block out, the heaviest on the transit center side. Their tactical team would move in from that side, the widest part of the yard and crescent around the parking lot, forcing any law enforcement activity into the narrower end point of the triangular yard with a contingency of backup in the surrounding commercial parking lots.

"Can we guarantee bystanders will be out of the way?"

"Not completely," Levi said. "Not without tipping the traffickers off that something is up."

"But," Matt interjected, "it is the end of the commercial portion of the rail line and the last transport of the week. We're hoping for light."

"Or," Kwan said, "it could be heavy because it's the last train out."

"We can't call Withers to find out," Marsh said, anticipating her next question. "They're on the take from Orchard."

"Can you get the manifests from the shipping company?"

"I may have a contact."

"Do it." She split a glance between Levi and Matt. "Adjust agent presence accordingly. What's the plan for Orchard?"

"Once they know we're on to them," Levi said, "they'll start destroying records if they haven't already. I'd suggest Alyssa and Will lead a second team on their offices, ready to go in as soon as we have the victims safe and the traffickers secure."

"How do you know they're not already on to you? Their lackeys were arrested and arraigned."

"They might be. But we were careful in all those filings to only mention the embezzlement at Celome."

"And the fact they tried to run you over with a car," Marsh interjected, still not able to get that nightmare completely out of his head. Speaking of nightmares… "Can you get us a sealed search warrant?"

Kwan cocked a brow. Marsh held her stare. "Get me the paperwork," she said after another moment. "I'll make it happen." She pointed at the papers on the table. "I want op details by the end of the day—on the rail yard and Orchard —and spec that shit out to within an inch of your lives— contingencies, collateral, backups. I want clean ops and collars this time."

"Yes, ma'am," Levi said as he and Matt gathered up the materials on the table. They were to the door before Levi seemed to realize Marsh wasn't on his heels. He shot a worried glance over his shoulder.

"I'll catch up," Marsh said with a nod. They'd talked about filling her in completely, and Levi and Matt had left it to his discretion. He offered Levi as confident a smile as he could muster.

Levi was reluctant to leave, but at Kwan's cleared throat behind them, he moved on, and Marsh closed the door.

"Tell me about the warrant," Kwan said, resting against her desk. She knew him too well.

And vice versa. He stayed far enough back so the visitor chairs were between them. Safe from her striking distance. "We have to do this without alerting Bell."

She struck the desk instead, smacking it with her palm. "Goddamnit, Nerd, I knew—"

"Julia."

"Nope!" She waggled a finger in the air in front of him. "Do not play that card unless it's a last resort. We're not there yet, are we?"

He pressed his lips together.

"Shit." She curled her fingers around the desk's edge. "Why do we need to keep Bell in the dark?"

"Because if he knows, word of our op might get back to the traffickers."

"Fuck." She hung her head, realization dawning, relief and anger colliding, same as they had for Marsh when he'd connected the dots. "The operation earlier this month?"

"Might not have been me that fucked that one up after all."

She lifted her head slowly, suddenly looking her age. Shoulders slumped, skin more fair, stress lines deeper like she was fighting the same ever-present headache he did. "Spec it out with as many people as you need but no more. Coordinate tactical and gear with Sandy Taylor. Tell her to run everything through me for approvals. We can trust her. For comms—"

"There's a cyber agent, Farmer, who could be an asset for us on this."

"He's good. Work it up."

"Feels like old times."

"That's not necessarily a good thing." She pushed off her desk and circled to her chair, slumping into it. "Whatever you have on Bell, is that what pushed Amanda over the edge into cooperating?"

He nodded. "Still working out how to present that."

"You didn't obtain it illegally, did you?"

"Nope, but it still might land my ass in a sling."

TWENTY-SEVEN

THE FRONT DOOR opened and closed, and before Levi could finish washing the pressure cooker pot, David and his snark entered the room. "Oh," he drawled in an almost perfect imitation of his grandmother. "You two are home for once?" Then quickly changed his tone. "Is that fried chicken I smell?" He tried to sneak between the island and fridge to peek at the crispy golden pieces Marsh was removing from the dutch oven on the stove, but Taco was taking up all the real estate in case any tasty bits hit the ground. The greyhound blockade delayed him long enough for reality—and suspicion—to set in. Arms crossed, he leaned a hip against the edge of the island. "What's going on?"

Levi dropped the stainless-steel pot back into the cooker. "An apology for leaving you to fend for yourself the past few days."

"The fridge was packed."

"That was my apology." Marsh removed the last piece

of chicken, stacking it on the serving plate with the others and sliding the plate onto the bar. "For beating you in our last chess game and for not starting another."

Sufficiently intrigued by Marsh's gastronomic bribery, David shuffled Taco to the other side of the gate, then climbed onto a stool and reached for a piece of chicken. "Work stuff?"

Levi popped his knuckles with the dishrag. "Yes, and manners. Wait for plates."

From Levi's other side, Marsh promptly picked up a drumstick and gnawed through it, garbling a "Why?" around his messy bite, effectively ruining any chance David wouldn't do the same.

Rolling his eyes, Levi retrieved plates and cutlery for himself and the heathens, then, using a potholder, removed the cast iron skillet of scalloped potatoes from the oven. He waggled a finger at both of them. "Do not touch that with your bare hands. We do not have time for an ER visit."

Dual pouts kept Levi laughing all the way to his stool between them. "I see what you did here," David said once everyone had loaded their plates. "But at least it's a tasty distraction."

"One of my best friend's, Sean," Marsh said, "spent a good chunk of his life in North Carolina. His husband and wife are from there. Picked up some of his tricks." He waved the rest of his drumstick in the air. "And I didn't have time to make proper barbecue."

"As in pulled pork? You know how?"

"I'm from Texas." He grabbed another piece of chicken off the plate. "I know how to handle a smoker. Would rather use it for a brisket—"

"That," David said, and at Levi's glare, added, "Yes, please."

Marsh chuckled. "You got it. This weekend."

Brisket sounded heavenly, and the poor neglected smoker outside needed some love and attention, but it was impossible not to wonder if Marsh would even be around this weekend. Not because Levi thought they couldn't handle the operation tomorrow. Yes, there would be risks, which was part of the talk he and Marsh were buttering David up for, but Levi believed in his team. So much so that he felt more confident than ever that they'd have the traffickers behind bars tomorrow. And then what happened? Would Marsh officially get his case back? Would he go back to Europe? Would Levi go with him to help? Or would Marsh want to work that by himself? Would they start the divorce proceedings?

"Uh-oh," David said. "What's that face for?"

Levi put down his fork and wiped his hands with his napkin. "Need you to start your weekend tomorrow."

"O-kay."

"At Mom and Dad's place."

"Why?" There was the whine Levi was expecting. "Can't you just pack the fridge and leave me here again? All of my sh—stuff is here."

"One, we don't know how long we're going to be, and two, it's for your own safety."

Snarky teenager left the building, David's eyes widening and his skin blanching, his freckles in high relief. "What's going on?"

"There's an operation tomorrow."

"Are you going to be in danger?"

"Every—"

David's gaze shot to Marsh, his tone as hard as his green eyes. "You promised not to let him get hurt."

That wasn't exactly what Marsh had promised—*he'd* promised not to hurt Levi—but it seemed Marsh wasn't splitting hairs either. "And I plan to keep that promise," he said. "But in order to do so, we both need to know you're safe."

Levi reached out and pried free the napkin David was about to shred into his potatoes, then squeezed his son's hand to emphasize the importance of his words. "And I'll feel better knowing you're there with Mom and Dad too."

David looked away, and Levi moved to slide off his stool and comfort his son, but then Marsh's hand landed on his thigh, startling him in place. Long enough for David to swallow and draw up his composure again. "You'll call or text me when you're safe?"

"Of course."

David withdrew his hand, pushed away his plate, and stood. "I'm sorry. Not hungry anymore."

This time Levi did move, and Marsh let him. "David," Levi said as he rounded the corner of the island.

"I'll come back for it," his son said with a step back. "I just need to"—he flapped a hand in the air like he was trying to grab the word that escaped him—"process." Then he turned to go.

Every muscle in Levi's body screamed to follow, his heart loudest of all.

He didn't have to.

David spun on his heel and lunged Levi's direction, hurling himself into his arms. "I know you're good at what you do, I just... With Mom gone..."

"I know." Levi curled his arms around him, burying his

nose in ginger curls. Stayed that way until David's breaths grew less ragged. "We'll keep you updated. I promise."

David hugged him a moment longer, then drew back... and launched himself at Marsh. "Thank you for the chicken." His words sounded as choked as Levi felt, witnessing a startled yet moved Marsh wrap his big arms around his son, graciously embracing him as if David were his own, making him feel safe.

"Wait until you try the brisket."

"It's a deal." David stepped back, sniffled a couple times, then chin down as if embarrassed by his show of emotion but hungry enough to still grab his plate, slipped out through the gate, Taco trailing behind him. Once his door closed, Levi turned toward the bar and let it take his weight, feeling more than he could handle settle on his shoulders, on his heart.

"Let it out," Marsh said from close behind him, then circled his waist with those same big arms that had comforted David. He leaned back against Marsh and let the ragged breaths out—short of sobs, dry of tears, but like he was running a marathon in elevation and couldn't catch his breath. "Breathe with me." Marsh lengthened his breaths, and once Levi's were in sync, inched a hand under his tee and splayed it over his abdomen.

Drawing up a memory—a fantasy—so fast Levi almost lost his breath again. "We can't—"

"I know." He nuzzled behind his ear. Inhaled. "Just want to hold you. Feel the warmth of you."

Oh.

Levi didn't object to the calming warmth against his back, against his belly. He ran a hand over Marsh's forearms stretched around him, the dark hairs tickling his fingertips, his senses. The edges of his fantasies he had no business delving into right now. But was the window for those fantasies to become reality closing? "I'm as terrified for this op to go right as I am for it to go wrong."

Marsh drew him closer. "Me too."

"Are you going to be here to cook him brisket this weekend?"

"Yes." He unwound an arm, lifted a hand, and used it to grasp Levi's chin, angling it so Levi could see into his eyes, could see the same banked fantasies darkening them now. "And once he's in his cave, passed out in a food coma, I'm going to kiss his father like I've wanted to since I first laid eyes on him."

Marsh teased the corner of his mouth with his thumb, and Levi turned into the touch, into his palm, chasing the promised heat. "Why can't you kiss me now?"

"I want to, Levi, so fucking much, but before we go there, we need to have a conversation about where this goes." He lowered his forehead against Levi's and his hand over Levi's chest. "Where your heart is and who it's with if I've got any chance of salvaging my own."

There was no way Marsh didn't feel the thump beneath his palm. Was that not answer enough? It fucking terrified Levi—the prospect of putting himself out there again, of losing someone he could see himself coming to care about as much as he'd cared about Kristin—but fuck if his heart wasn't already halfway there.

Marsh shifted him back against his chest, his hold secure as he rested his chin on Levi's shoulder. "If that conversation goes the way I want it to, if I kiss you, I can't guarantee we'll get much sleep, and right now, those trafficking victims need our attention more than our dicks do."

Levi choked on a laugh, the sound bubbling out of him, louder when Marsh nipped at the tendon in his neck.

Was he terrified? Yes.

Enough to put the brakes on? What was it Marsh liked to say... Time to cowboy up.

TWENTY-EIGHT

WAITING in a building lobby across the street from the Withers Escondido rail yard, Levi felt the rumble of the approaching train beneath his feet, heard the chug of the engine, the clank of the wheels, and the whine of the brakes.

"Engine and five cars," Agent Farmer radioed.

"Matches the info from my source," Marsh replied from beside Levi. "Should be the last one."

As it came around the bend in the track, the train appeared outside the building's west-side windows. Levi could see straight through from the lobby into the vacant retail space where another team of agents kept eyes on the train. The agents in the cleared-out office space to Levi's left continued to monitor the rail yard. In the block behind the building, two more teams were stationed on each corner, with local police presence beefed up too, ready to clear streets and provide civilian protection if needed. At the narrow, southern end of the rail yard, Matt waited in the communications van with Agent Farmer and a third team.

It was more people involved than any of them wanted, especially the ASAC, but it was the bare minimum they needed to secure the area and to have a real chance of rescuing the women lured there by Amanda's false promises.

"We've got eyes on Claire and Keira," Farmer reported. "They just stepped off the light rail at the transit center. Headed for the south platform exit."

Headed Levi's direction. This was going to be the hardest part of the entire operation. Watching two victims walk right past him. Waiting for them to make contact with the traffickers, for the commission of a crime, before Levi's team could act. If Levi lost them this time, he'd only have himself to blame.

Marsh clicked through security feeds on the hacked reception computer with one hand and skirted the other under the bottom of Levi's flak jacket, into the groove at the small of Levi's back. "We'll get them out of this safely," he reassured Levi as Claire and Keira traversed their block.

"Cab pulling into the parking lot here," Matt said, followed by Farmer's confirmation that the taxi's passengers were the other two women from the forged IDs. "They're crossing to the parking lot on the other side of the tracks."

The same place Claire and Keira were headed, crossing the street and walking down the sidewalk just outside the rail yard's west-side fence.

"Teams, report," Levi ordered.

Each position radioed their status, the only anomaly a company happy hour overflowing into one of the parking lots the direction of the transit center.

Marsh flicked through surveillance feeds until he found

the northeast facing one. Sure enough, folks were leaving one of the buildings, crowding around a ping pong table set up in the parking lot. Directly between their building's block and the transit center. "Even more reason to make sure they don't divert that direction," Marsh said.

Leaving them a very narrow window in Matt's direction, at the southern point of the triangular-shaped rail yard. In a push, they could chase the traffickers due east, but any such pursuit would have to be on foot, the water filtration plant in the adjacent lot too close for high-speed car chases to navigate. Levi preferred to be on foot. They'd have the advantage barring unknown variables, of which there was still one outstanding on the victims' side. "Anyone got eyes on Maria?"

"Negative," each team replied.

"If she shows," Marsh said off comm, "we'll get her out too."

"We've got a Sprinter van approaching," Farmer radioed.

"Showtime," Marsh said, a counter to Matt's more circumspect, "Not their usual setup."

"But what Amanda told them to expect," Levi said. "Also less obvious in broad daylight. Farmer, alert the PD. Get them ready to stop traffic in case we need to move."

Farmer confirmed while, beside Levi, Marsh suddenly patted his vest's pockets, eventually yanking his phone out of one. Cursing, he angled it Levi's direction so he could read the one-word text from Kwan. **FUBAR.**

Levi added his curse to the mix, then mouthed a one-word question to Marsh. *Bell?* Marsh nodded. "On alert," Levi ordered his teams. "Move the PD into position. Close surrounding streets. Farmer, direct Oscar team to get ready." Will and Alyssa were outside Orchard Investment's headquarters, warrant in hand, ready to seize computers and records.

The Sprinter van parked in the rail yard lot where the four women had gathered. They were out of Levi's direct line of sight but in view of the comm truck's camera's, a feed streamed directly to the monitor at Marsh's command. A sharply dressed man—white, late twenties, brown hair, average build—stepped out of the van, balancing a tray of champagne and glasses.

In character.

"He's armed," Matt said. "Bulge under his coat. Lower back."

"Anyone else in the van?" Marsh asked.

"Driver behind the wheel."

"Plus another in the main part of the van," Farmer said. "Heat signatures show them close to the door but behind the tinted class."

Three total. Levi's team had more manpower, but the traffickers had wheels and firepower they wouldn't hesitate to use. And hostages—four of them, one of whom was starting to object. Keira sniffed the champagne, then paused before sipping, unlike the other three women who'd downed their bubbly in one gulp. Keira thrust the glass back at the suited man, and when he wouldn't take it, began to animatedly argue with him. All while the other women started to wobble and lean against each other for balance.

"Wine was drugged," Marsh said.

"First position," Levi told his teams. He and Marsh rounded the reception desk, drawing weapons and pausing at the lobby's front doors. The teams in the spaces on either side of Levi did the same. Everyone waiting for his signal.

Keira threw down her glass, spun on her heel, and got one step before a second man emerged from the van. Also white, he was twice the suit's size and not half as nicely dressed. He grabbed Keira by the arm and roughly hauled her toward the van. She shouted and struggled, aided by the other women who had caught on to something amiss. The suit rushed to corral them, reaching behind his back for his gun.

Levi opened his mouth to give the go order when all hell broke loose, Maria staggering out from between the water filtration tanks and startling the traffickers. The suit swung his gun arm her direction and fired. Screaming, Keira broke loose from her attacker's hold and ran the opposite direction, toward Matt's team in the adjacent parking lot, the other women hot on her heels while Maria bolted back the direction of the tanks. In the rail yard, the getaway driver cranked the truck and wildly swung the direction of the north exit, exactly the direction Levi couldn't let them go.

"Bravo Team, go!" Levi ordered, sending Matt's team to intercept and secure the victims headed their direction.

"Alpha, Charlie, Delta, converge."

Marsh shoved open the lobby door, sprinting across the cleared street, Levi on his six, continuing to give orders on the move. "Echo, Foxtrot, second position. Oscar is a go."

As soon as the entire rail yard came into view and Levi saw that Matt's team was closer to the victims than the van, Levi shouted, "FBI! Stop," alerting the traffickers to their presence and distracting them from Matt's incoming team. The gunman swiveled, firing erratically, and Levi thanked all that was holy that Marsh wasn't wearing one of his giant hats today. Too easy a target. As it were, Marsh was already the largest person in an FBI windbreaker bearing down on the scene.

And intimidating enough, with a line of agents converging behind him, to make the traffickers rethink their plan. The more casually dressed man hauled ass back into the van, the suit not far behind but not fast enough. Launching off one foot, Marsh landed against the suit's back, wrapped his arms around his shoulders, and using his weight as leverage, wrestled him to the ground.

Clearing a path for Levi and the other agents to the truck, which hit the gas and barreled straight for them.

♟♙♟♙♙♙♙♟♙♙

MARSH WAS REALLY FUCKING tired of people trying to run his husband over. Thank fuck Levi was fast enough, both times, to dive out of the way, but like before, Marsh didn't get a chance to even check him over before Levi was back up and running after the suspects. Which was probably why Marsh went a bit rough on Mr. Suit when he tried to buck Marsh off and fight back. Who the fuck did this jackass think he was? Yes, that leap to take him down had made Marsh feel all of his forty-six years, but he'd wrestled bulls ten times the guy's size before. Hauling Mr. Suit onto his back, Marsh brought a swift elbow down onto the bridge of his nose, and then, when the idiot lifted his arms to cover his face, brought a second elbow down into his gut. Low enough not to break anything but in just the right spot to steal his breath, to make Mr. Suit curl inward and surrender. Marsh flipped him back onto his front, wrenched his arms behind his back, and slapped the cuffs around his wrists.

With Levi and the Charlie and Delta teams chasing after the two remaining suspects, Marsh called over the closest member of Matt's Bravo team. "He's secure. Get him to the truck."

Then Marsh was up and chasing after Levi and the suspects too. "Bishop, where are you?"

"In pursuit on foot. Running north along the west side of the staging building. Suspects on wheels an alley over. They're headed toward the transit—Fucking hell!"

"What the hell, Foxtrot?" Farmer echoed. "You just let them through."

"Direct order from SAC Bell," an agent replied. "Victims are secure. Suspect apprehended. Op is over."

Fucking Bell. "I'll go an alley over to the east," Marsh reported. "Will move to intercept." Except he wasn't fast enough on foot to make that happen. At the next cross street where cars and pedestrians had been diverted, he flashed his badge to the officers there and commandeered the first police car in sight. "I've got wheels," he radioed. "Farmer, give me the clearest path to herd the suspects away from the transit center."

"You've got the transit center parking lot, another to the west across the street, and then the next block north is the abandoned cement factory."

"There, Marsh," Levi said. "Herd them there if you can cut them off. They're almost to the transit center inter-section."

Marsh gunned the jacked-up SUV, shooting ahead, mentally thanking the local cops for at least doing their jobs and keeping the streets clear. He shot out from the alley just in time to catch the Sprinter van doing the same on the other side of the block. The van started to turn right, until Marsh hit the horn and flashers. The Sprinter van careened to the left instead, tilting on two wheels and barely making the turn into the parking lot across from the transit center.

Marsh wrenched his own vehicle the same direction and sped down the street... and nearly missed hitting Levi himself when he and two other agents came barreling down the other road. He swerved right, the SUV rocking up on two wheels, same as the Sprinter van had. It was a nauseating few seconds in which gravity didn't seem to exist, then it blessedly returned, the SUV plunking down on four wheels again, and Marsh burning rubber to catch up to the Sprinter van while it was in the same parking lot, while Levi and company trailed on foot along the sidewalk on the other side of the parking lot fence.

"Farmer!" Levi shouted. "Are we clear of any civilians now?"

"Clear," Farmer confirmed.

"Marsh, hit the gas and give the van a tap. If you can get it to spin left, we're close enough to shoot out the wheels and rock it over."

"Roger that." He shifted up a gear, gunned the SUV, and its cage grill connected with the Sprinter's fender. Marsh gave the SUV a little more gas and watched the back end of the van start to fishtail. He slammed on the brakes, then slammed the SUV into reverse, speeding backward out of the way and giving Levi and his teams room to work.

They made fast work of it, both tires on the left side shot out before the driver could get an elbow out the window, much less an arm and weapon. And once the van started to topple, he needed both hands to try—and fail—to right it. The van skidded a good ten feet on its side across the parking lot, slamming to a halt against the hedge-lined fence at the far end.

Marsh caught up to Levi and his team outside the van, weapons drawn, sirens screaming in the background, as reinforcements converged. "FBI!" Levi shouted. "Come out with your hands up."

Gunfire erupted from inside the van, and all the agents outside dove for cover, Marsh dragging Levi with him behind the SUV. The flurry was brief... and contained. Inside the van. When no other sounds came from the van, when there was no response to Levi's shouts of "FBI!" and "Come out with your hands up," they approached slowly and carefully peeked inside the front windshield. Their two remaining suspects were dead.

TWENTY-NINE

"THAT'S ALL the accounts on my list," Agent Farmer said as he rolled back from his workstation. "Shut down."

Marsh stood from behind the laptop he'd been pushing equally hard. "And that's all the ones on mine. Shut down." Farmer extended a fist his direction for a bump, and Marsh met his knuckles midair. "Nice work today. In the field and on this." This being the list of Orchard bitcoin accounts Frederick had provided, all of them now officially seized.

"Thanks for bringing me in."

"Go ahead to the war room and give them the good news. I'm going to hit the head, then I'll be right behind you."

Farmer stood and strode out of the room, moving at a far quicker clip than Marsh, who needed to stop pretending he was Farmer's age in the field. He snagged two ibuprofen packets from the cyber bullpen stash, rode the elevator down a floor, then ducked into the restroom. He took a leak, washed his hands, and had just popped the pain pills with a handful of disgusting San Diego water—the only bad thing about this place—when the restroom door opened.

The furthest thing from bad slipped inside.

Marsh finished wiping his hands, tossed the paper towels into the trash, and opened his arms. Levi walked into them without hesitation, winding his own around Marsh's waist, tucking his face into the crook of Marsh's neck, and inhaling deep. He fit so well there, as well like this, front to front, as back to front, the way Marsh was so fond of holding him at home. *Home*, he was ready to get there with Levi, had been ready hours ago, and yet they still had hours of work ahead of them.

"Did you text David?"

Levi nodded. "Mom will drop him off in the morning." Levi nuzzled closer, and Marsh decided he liked this fit better. "I thought you were going over in that SUV."

"I thought I was going to hit you *after* I watched that Sprinter van almost hit you." Marsh left one arm around Levi's waist and coasted his other hand up and down Levi's spine, soaking in the warmth and strength that had likewise been at risk but was safe now in his arms.

"Twice in a month."

"Let's not make a habit of that."

Lifting his head, Levi skirted his cheek along Marsh's jaw, his hands up Marsh's chest. Heat bloomed under his touch and in his voice. "I need…"

"Not here."

"Marsh." The whine wasn't as full blown as David's, but it was reminiscent enough to make Marsh snicker.

Smiling, he drew back and gently cupped Levi's cheek. "I need it too, but when I kiss you for the first time, it will not be in the FBI bathroom."

He almost went back on his word when Levi shifted, angling his face to kiss his palm, but Farmer sticking his head through the bathroom door saved him the backpedal. "You two need to get to the war room ASAP."

They were halfway there when Bell's voice boomed from inside, loud enough to be heard across the floor. "Who authorized a raid on Orchard Investments?"

"I did," Kwan answered. Marsh was hustling through bullpen desks behind Levi, wasn't to the war room yet where he could see her, but he was sure Kwan was standing tall and straight, standing behind the decisions they'd made and the operations they'd conducted.

"Without getting my approval?"

"I don't need your approval."

They entered the room just as Matt, at Kwan's side, replied, "We've got a confession from the trafficker in lockup, a confession from his accomplices, and a clear money trail. Right back to Orchard."

"You've got the word of criminals," Bell replied.

"Exactly."

"All for what? To run a local business into the ground?"

"To save five women," Levi interjected.

"Five illegals," Bell spat, and if not for Levi shifting in front of him, Marsh would have probably hauled off and hit the man. "This is insubordination."

"Respectfully, sir," Marsh started more calmly. Only for the SAC to react in the exact opposite manner, bearing down on Marsh. "And what are you doing here? You're not supposed to be anywhere near this case."

"While I continued to work on your case, I offered my husband and his team support on theirs."

Bell cringed at the word *husband*. Let his disgust out on a curse. "Bullshit!"

Marsh idly wondered at which part because Bell's objections, all of them, were complete and utter bullshit.

"Your transfer request is denied," the SAC railed on. "You're off my identity theft case, and you're sure as fuck off this one. Pack your shit and get out of here. And you three"—he gestured at Levi, Matt, and Kwan—"are suspended without pay."

"On what grounds?" Matt exclaimed.

"I already told you. Insubordination." He grabbed the conference room phone and dialed someone. His secretary, Marsh guessed, given the barked orders that followed. "Get me OPR on the line." While he waited, he pointed at Levi again. "I will make sure you do not set foot in this building again until your husband is gone for good."

With Levi apparently stunned silent, Marsh started to object on his behalf. Kwan's hand on his forearm silenced him. "Levi's team can handle this. *I* can handle this." Her eyes cut to Levi, and Marsh's gaze followed. There was a green hue to his pale face and the up and down movement of his chest, the rapid puffs of his breaths, were erratic at best. Marsh didn't argue with her whispered "Get him out of here."

Levi was about to blow or collapse, neither of which he needed others to witness. Marsh could be there for him, bear the brunt of either outcome in private, then Marsh would pack his bags and leave. He couldn't keep risking Levi's life and job. He had too many people who loved him, needed him, and he was too damn good at his job to lose it. People like those women today needed him. Marsh had to leave. That's what Levi needed more than him.

THIRTY

LEVI COULDN'T BELIEVE his eyes. The agent who wouldn't quit, the cowboy who'd wrestled steers, the hacker who'd managed to get ahead of the criminals that had eluded Levi for eighteen months, the man who'd put a goddamn ring on Levi's finger because he was so determined to solve their cases and get justice for those they'd lost was packing his bags, fucking quitting before the mission was complete. "You're just going to leave?"

"You heard the SAC." They were the first words Marsh had spoken since they'd left the office. He'd tried in the elevator on their way out of the building, but Levi had shushed him with a raised hand, unable to hear it then, unwilling to snap at the person who least deserved his anger. Without another word, Marsh had driven them home, let Levi into the house, and kept watch from the patio door while Levi leashed Taco and left for a walk.

To return home to the unbelievable.

Marsh removed his unbuttoned dress shirt, shoved it

into a duffel, and zipped the bag. "I told you I would do everything in my power to minimize the risk to your job."

"Too late!"

Marsh cringed, and Levi immediately regretted his tone, regretted that it sounded like anger directed at Marsh instead of at SAC Bell and the criminals who were putting all their lives and jobs at risk.

"I can fix it." Marsh skirted past Levi, out of the guest bedroom and into the adjacent bath. "I'll leave, cancel the transfer request, keep investigating EC on my own." His back and shoulders rippled under his white T-shirt, tense at holding himself in check, every motion jerky yet efficient like he was fighting other movements he wanted to make instead. He packed his items into his toiletry kit, erasing all traces that he'd been there, had started to settle, had lost some of his transient neatness. Exactly as Levi had wanted —to make Marsh feel at home. A home he was now leaving. "I'll start the annulment paperwork when I get back to Europe. We never fucked so…"

Not what Levi wanted, the very words souring his stomach. Marsh was lashing out, responding to what he perceived as Levi's first strike. Levi struck again, unintentionally, before he could catch himself or his tone. "That's TV land. You know that's not how it legally works."

Marsh didn't reply. He zipped his toiletry kit and pushed past Levi back into the bedroom. Face turned away, he shoved the leather kit into his other duffel and zipped that one too.

Levi's stomach sank, withering hopes dragging it to the floor. "Is that what you want?" Levi's voice wobbled, his knees too, and he had to catch himself against the dresser, a lamp teetering precariously.

Marsh's gaze shot to his, and it was so full of agony Levi gasped. This was killing him too, the pain and fear right there in his dark eyes, in the words that seemed to lodge in his throat, coming out thick and rough. "Of course it's not. But what I want isn't the point." He grabbed the duffel straps in one hand, hefted the bags over his shoulder, and withdrew a folded piece of paper from his back pocket. He opened it on the dresser next to Levi's hand—a check for three times as much as the first one he'd given Levi. "In case me leaving doesn't fix this, that should take care of you and David long enough for you to get back on your feet. If it's not enough, contact Brax. He'll be able to reach me, and I'll get you more."

More?

That check was *more* than a year's worth of salary. More than enough to keep him and David afloat. But all the money in the world wasn't what Levi needed. After three weeks, he understood better what he and David needed, and today, watching that SUV almost topple over with Marsh inside it, watching now as Marsh packed his bags, Levi's understanding was reinforced.

He knew exactly what—*who*—he needed.

He just had to ask.

Finding his legs again, he stepped in front of Marsh and blocked the door. "I don't need a check. I need a partner."

"You have Matt."

"Here, Marsh." He spread his arms wide, indicating the house around them. "I need a partner here." Then folded both hands over his heart. "And here."

Tortured eyes held Levi's, a battle raging in them between what Marsh thought he should do and what he wanted to do. But there didn't need to be a war at all; the two sides weren't at odds. Leaving one hand over his own heart, Levi reached out the other and laid it over Marsh's. "Me and my heart are right here. Where are you and yours?"

The duffel bags hit the floor.

"With you," Marsh declared, and with his freed hands, roughly grasped Levi's face and slammed their mouths together. Holding him, forcing his jaw open, plunging his tongue between Levi's lips and plundering his mouth.

Exactly the way Levi needed it. Exactly the way he'd fantasized more times than he could count over the past few weeks. Groaning, he pushed up against Marsh's body and got the push back he craved, all the way to the bedroom wall, his back hitting it hard, his head cushioned by Marsh's hand in his hair. Pressed between Marsh's big body and the wall, Levi hadn't felt so safe—so fucking turned on—in he couldn't remember how long.

He hooked a leg over Marsh's hip and thrust his cock against Marsh's, both of them well on their way to erect. Marsh gasped, and Levi took advantage, teasing and tasting the mouth that had tempted him from first smirk. He didn't mind the taste of coffee when it was on Marsh's tongue. Didn't mind the tickle of his beard or Marsh's hand clutching his thigh. Certainly didn't mind the greedy moan that rumbled out of Marsh's throat and down his own.

Levi did, however, mind when Marsh ripped his mouth away. He dove in for another kiss, and got a mouth full of beard, Marsh dodging the kiss. "We're supposed to have a conversation."

"We just did." Levi withdrew his hands from where they'd wandered under Marsh's shirt and framed his red-stained cheeks, the blush making his bronze skin glow.

"I've wanted you since you slid into that chair across from me at dinner. Needed you since before then. Need you in my heart and in my home and in my bed. I need you to fuck me, Marsh. I'm asking. Will you give it to me? Will you give me what you promised last weekend?"

"Jesus," Marsh cursed, forehead falling against Levi's.

"Not Jesus, just Bishop, and I'll take that as a yes."

Marsh's smile collided with his.

♟♙♟♙♙♙♙♟♙♙

THAT SMILE TURNED into a smirk when Marsh hefted Levi into his arms and Levi yelped. "What are you doing?"

"I need more real estate for everything I promised you." More real estate being the king-size bed in Levi's room. He made it across the catwalk with a handsy Levi feeling him up and nipping his neck the whole way. Reaching the bed by some miracle, he put one then the other knee to the mattress and lowered Levi onto his back. He stretched out above him and gazed down at the remarkable man he couldn't walk away from. Pale skin flushed, plump lips parted, blue eyes fiery with lust and conviction. With the confidence to ask for what he needed.

What Marsh needed just as desperately.

There was no way Marsh could refuse him.

He brought his lips back to the bruised ones uttering his name and kissed the daylights out of Levi, parting only for breaths and curses, until it became clear their grinding hips were going to rob them both of what they needed before long.

Marsh sat back on his haunches and shucked his undershirt. Levi's gaze shot to his chest and raked over it with heat that scorched through Marsh's veins. "You have two minutes to finish undressing me before the hard and rough portion of the festivities begins."

Levi grinned, that fucking dimple making a long-awaited reappearance. "I only need one." Fast as lightning, Marsh's belt was off and zipper lowered, then so too was Marsh, bucked onto his back so Levi could yank free his shoes and socks, followed by his pants and boxers, Marsh's phone in his pocket making a *thunk* of an exclamation point as it hit the floor. Done with Marsh, Levi used his other minute to strip himself with delightfully zero modesty. He climbed back onto the bed, nimble and graceful, and Marsh idly wondered how many seconds, how many minutes, how many days it would take to kiss every inch of his rosy skin, every sculpted muscle, every freckle exposed by the moonlight shining in through the giant windows.

"Marsh?"

His gaze shot to the blue one looking down at him, a hint of uncertainty starting to creep into Levi's expression. Marsh couldn't have any of that. He ran a hand up Levi's closest thigh, curled it around his hip, and squeezed. "I nicknamed you Wolfy because, like this, your blue eyes glowing in the moonlight, you look like one of those hot wolf shifters from the romance novels I used to read on base. You're fucking beautiful."

Doubt fled, and Levi's smile returned. Touch feather-light, he traced a path with his fingers down Marsh's sternum, over his abs, around his belly button, and into the coarse trail of hair below, fanning out over his pelvis. Marsh thrust toward the touch. "You're pretty fucking beautiful yourself, Mount Cowboy." He dipped his fingers lower, avoiding where Marsh wanted them most, where he needed them least if this was going to last. Cupping his balls with one hand, Levi stretched and wove the fingers of the other into Marsh's hair, holding him at both ends as he bent over and kissed Marsh's chest, right over his heart, lingering there until he angled his face and glanced up at Marsh, his eyes flashing white hot.

Levi's words brought all Marsh's banked fantasies to life. "Now fucking ride me."

Marsh didn't hesitate, surging up and snaking an arm around Levi's waist. He hauled him in for a quick rough kiss, needing a taste of beauty and fire, before he proceeded to do all the things he'd promised Levi.

Flipping him onto his stomach and shoving one leg wide, wedging a knee under his thigh to lever his ass up, and reaching a hand around to his cock. Stroking him while he slid his own dick along the crease of Levi's ass. Riding, building them both as Levi fucked his hand and the bed.

Easing off when Levi was on the pleading edge of orgasm, sliding down his body and sucking kisses to each vertebra until he reached Levi's firm, round ass cheeks, spreading them with his hands and teasing his rim before he speared his tongue inside his hole.

Spreading his own knees, levering up as much as he could so he didn't come by rutting his own stiff prick against the mattress with every grunt and groan Levi made, every "Marsh, please," that fell like a prayer from his lips.

Stretching up and over Levi's body, grabbing the lube out of the bedside table, and tattooing his own litany of "I need to" and "I need you" across the back of Levi's shoulders as he finished working Levi open with his slick fingers.

Pausing with his tip at Levi's hole, checking for Levi's

consent one last time before pushing into his tight heat bare. Shivering at the overwhelming sensation before gathering himself to give Levi what he'd promised. Planting a hand on Levi's back, one on the mattress by his head, and driving into him hard and rough.

Shouting when Levi shifted, allowing Marsh's cock to sink deeper, then exploding when, with one flick of his tongue against the tip of Marsh's thumb, Levi catapulted Marsh over the edge.

♟♙♟♙♙♙♟♙♟

AS A SATED Marsh splayed out on top of him, sank deeper into him, Levi had to make room to reach down and clasp the base of his dick, the urge to come damn near impossible to ignore. Marsh was so hot, so heavy, so all-encompassing, so everything Levi needed.

His dick throbbed in his hand.

"Marsh, I need to come."

Warm lips trailed across his shoulder blades. "I need to finish giving you what I promised."

Levi would settle for the orgasm, but then Marsh eased his dick out of him, only long enough to make room for his fingers, gliding them through the come that leaked out of him. Recalling all that was promised, wanting it worse now than he had a week ago, Levi didn't wait for Marsh to flip him over. Jostling Marsh off his back, he flopped onto his, elevated his ass with a pillow, and spread his legs. He stroked his aching cock, slicking it with precome and leaking on his stomach.

"Fuck. Look at you." Marsh covered his hand, stroking

him together, picking up the pace, hard and rough the way Levi liked it. Letting his hand fall out from under Marsh's, Levi curled his fingers in the sheets and shoved his head back into the pillow, eyes scrunched closed in agony at holding himself back. Wanting the release as much as he wanted Marsh to keep denying him. Soaring higher with every "Not yet" Marsh kissed into his skin.

Marsh shifted, the bulk of him settling between Levi's spread legs, his rough cheeks scratching the insides of his thighs, teasing and torturing. "You're fucking perfect, Levi." Releasing Levi's cock, he aimed lower, fingers trailing over Levi's rim again, smearing the come leaking out of him, his tongue following in his fingers' wake, making Levi ache and writhe. He shoved a hand into Marsh's hair, grabbed at the thick strands, and held him there. Wanted him to stay there forever, the dirtiness of it all too perfect.

It was everything Levi needed, everything he'd missed since losing Kristin, failing to find it with anyone else. Not until this selfless man walked into his life and gave Levi a ring and everything he hadn't expected.

Marsh flattened his tongue against the underside of his balls, dragged it across his perineum, then up the length of his cock, flicking the bundle of nerves on the underside of his head. Circling, the heat of Marsh's breath threatened to swallow him whole, lips parting to—

"Stop!"

Marsh pulled off, gaze whipping to his. "What's wrong?"

"Nothing. Everything's right. I just need something more."

Unfolding from between his legs, Marsh shifted to

Levi's side, lying so his body touched the entire length of Levi's, his face nuzzled into the crook of Levi's neck. "Whatever you need, baby."

Levi rotated onto his side, bringing them front to front, and slung a leg over Marsh's hip. Taking Marsh's come-slick hand in his, he wrapped it around his cock. "Finish me like this." He scooted closer, mouths sharing air, sharing more if Levi had his way. "I want to feel your lips against mine when you tell me to come."

Marsh gave him a long, slow stroke. "You're more than I bargained for, Levi Bishop."

Levi thrust into his hand and brushed his lips against Marsh's. "But a good bargain, yeah?"

"The best."

"That's good," Levi panted as Marsh worked him harder, faster. "Because I feel like I got a steal. So much more than a smirking cowboy in a Stetson."

"If you let me," Marsh said, adding a twist on the next stroke, "I'll show you everything. Everything I can fucking give you. Every way I can fuck you."

Levi arched toward him, hissing a "Yes," wanting it all with Marsh. "Yes, please."

"I'll be the best for you too." He plunged his tongue into Levi's mouth, a dominating sweep, a jerky thrust against his thigh, a faltering stroke. Then so soft it brought tears to Levi's eyes. Marsh whispered the thing Levi needed to hear most against his lips. "Come."

And Levi surrendered to everything.

THIRTY-ONE

MARSH'S VIBRATING phone drew him out of slumber, out of Levi's arms and bed as he searched for the annoying disturbance. He tiptoed around the darkened room, searching the shadows cast by the dim light of dawn sneaking around the curtains' edges. Levi must have gotten up and pulled them at some point during the night. He considered the light again, then peeked at the clock. Six in the morning. Marsh had slept through the whole night— with the gorgeous man still lightly snoring in bed. Levi lay on his back, the sheet bunched around his waist, his face angled toward the rising sun, his dark blond hair a rumpled mess from Marsh's fingers and from his own abandon. God, he'd been amazing, surrendering every kiss, every grunt and groan, his orgasm and every inch of his body to Marsh. A body Marsh admired again now, his gaze drawn to Levi's left hand resting on his abs, to the ring on his fourth finger as it caught one of the creeping rays of light.

Marsh twirled the matching band around his own finger. He was falling—hard, fast, and deep—for his husband. More so than he ever had for Sean or Brax. Quickly nearing Patrick levels of attachment. Eclipsing anyone he'd ever been with in terms of desire. He'd never wanted anyone as much as he'd wanted Levi last night— hell, every day of the past three weeks. And again this morning, it seemed, his dick hardening as he raked his gaze over a resting Levi.

A real, well-deserved rest.

His phone vibrated again, threatening to destroy it.

"Are you going to keep staring?" Levi mumbled. Too late. Blue eyes flicked open partway, staring at Marsh from under hooded lids. "Or are you gonna answer the damn phone?"

Marsh palmed his cock through his boxers. "Maybe I'll just ignore it."

"Answer it, get rid of them, then get back in bed." Levi kicked aside the sheet, tented boxers on full display. Someone else was ready to go again too. "We've got an hour before David gets home."

Marsh chuffed. "Now who's giving orders?"

Levi grabbed his erection through the silk and bowed his back, his amazing body reaching toward Marsh.

For Marsh.

Marsh expedited his search. He found his pants in the corner, snatched his phone out of the pocket, and glanced at the screen. Two texts and a call from Agent Farmer. He hit the callback button and lowered himself onto the side of the bed. "Farmer, it's awfully—"

"Matt and Gail are in the hospital."

Marsh switched the phone to speaker. "Repeat that."

"Matt and Gail are at Scripps Mercy. An explosive device was delivered to Matt's rental this morning."

Levi rocketed up in bed, immediately awake. "What sort of explosive?"

"Small device. Relatively contained. Not as powerful as the one delivered to Bell."

"How powerful was the one delivered to Bell?" Marsh said.

"He's dead."

Levi lurched forward, swinging his legs around to hang off the bed, sitting shoulder to shoulder with Marsh. "He's dead?"

"The explosive was hidden inside a chess set." Farmer's gulp was audible. "The one from ASAC Kwan's office. When he opened it, the explosive detonated."

Levi stiffened, his wide-eyed gaze clashing with Marsh's. "Didn't you give her that chess set?"

Marsh nodded and forced words out around the fear forming a knot in his throat. "Where's Julia?"

"They arrested her an hour ago."

He breathed out the fear and inhaled anger. "She didn't do this."

Levi grasped his forearm, fingers pressing just shy of painful. Marsh turned his eyes back to Levi and found him that awful greenish shade of pale again. His voice was barely a whisper when he spoke. "Yours wasn't on the table when we got home last night."

"What about the package delivered to Matt? Was it—"

"A chess set. Looked new from the security footage."

Not his.

"There's one more thing," Farmer said, and Marsh barely bit back the *No!* on the tip of his tongue. How much bad news could one person deliver? "Greg and Amanda are also missing."

Levi's grip skidded down his forearm to his wrist. Became a vise. Like he was holding on for dear life. "They're eliminating everyone who knows the truth."

Meaning they were a target too.

"Farmer, get protection on Kwan, Matt, and Gail."

Letting him go, Levi rolled the opposite direction, to the other side of the bed, and yanked his phone off the charger. He scrambled back to Marsh's side, home security app opened. "No notifications. Nothing on the doorstep."

"Open the recorded feed," Marsh said as he tossed his own phone aside. "Rewind it back."

Levi opened the recording, and once the bar at the bottom appeared, slowly slid his thumb left across the screen, playing time backward. Nothing unusual appeared... until 4:50 a.m., when the time skipped to 4:48 a.m.

"Right there," Marsh said. "A minute's gone." He remembered that missing minute from the rail yard security feed. "Fuck, go back to the live feed."

The sound of the front door opening echoed from downstairs.

The front door did not open on-screen. Because, like at the rail yard three weeks ago, they weren't watching a live feed.

"Hey!" David shouted from the great room. "You guys up? Why was the chess set left on the front porch?"

Marsh shot off the bed, fear rocketing back to terrifying life, propelling him out of the room and down the stairs, while Levi bellowed from the balcony above. "David! Don't open it!"

Startled, David bobbled the box, the chess set slipping through his fingers.

The life Marsh had fallen asleep dreaming about—in this home, with his husband, with this amazing kid—slipping through his own.

He couldn't reach the box before it hit the ground and flew open.

"Levi, get back!" he yelled as he cleared the bottom step.

He snatched his Stetson off the newel where he'd left it last night, slung it across the floor in the direction of the falling box, then lunged for David, taking him over the nearest part of the sectional and with his free arm, grabbing the sectional piece and pulling it over them, a buffer for the impending explosion.

Which thank the fucking Lord never came.

Unless you counted David's explosive, "What the fuck is going on?" Marsh let the sectional piece go, and David shot to his feet, head on a swivel as his gaze bounced between him and Levi charging down the stairs. "And why the fuck did you come rushing out of my dad's room?"

Levi crashed into his son, arms circling David, holding him tight. Marsh checked that the chess set was closed and stable, cushioned in the crown of his hat, that Taco and Burrito were safely behind the gate, then joined his family, wrapping his arms around Levi and David and thanking all the saints for keeping them safe.

This time.

THIRTY-TWO

THE FRIDAY before July Fourth was a good day to fly out of McClellan-Palomar Airport. The single runway airport that catered to San Diego's one-percenters and their private jets was busy with executives returning home for the holiday, wealthy tourists flying in for a long weekend at the beach, and wealthy locals flying out to Vegas, Napa, and other destinations.

Perfect for an under-the-radar getaway.

Levi could hardly believe he was going to be on one of those private jets. Would rather it be for a vacation than fleeing to Marsh hadn't told him where, but that's where they were. Fleeing from the criminals who'd killed his boss, framed his supervisor, nearly killed his partner, and almost killed his son.

As they waited for Marsh to clear security, Levi tugged David close with an arm around his shoulder and dropped a kiss on his head. The fact that David didn't immediately shrug him off told Levi everything he needed to know about how his son was feeling. "It's going to be okay," he whispered.

Wary green eyes blinked up at him. "Don't lie to me."

Until that moment, Levi had thought losing Kristin was the hardest thing he'd ever been through. But losing his kid's trust was rivaling it for top honors. "I know a lot of things don't make sense right now. I know you're scared. I am too. I've never been more scared than when I saw that chess set in your hands this morning." David shivered, and Levi drew him closer. "But we're safe now, and we'll be even safer once we get on that plane."

"And then you'll explain?"

"What we can," Marsh said, joining them.

"Are you sure Brax is going to be able to get a gate?" Levi asked.

"I'm sure." Marsh jutted his chin at the parting crowd ten or so feet ahead, at the cadre of intimidating figures cutting a path through the concourse. At their helm was a petite woman with long blond hair, sharp features, ice-blue eyes, and a *get out of my fucking way* glare that had strangers hustling to obey. Which made the wink she cast Levi's direction as they passed all the more startling, so distracting Levi almost missed the note the person with a rainbow-colored mohawk slipped Marsh.

"Who was that?" Levi asked him, once the group was on the other side of security, on their way to exiting the concourse.

"Family," Marsh replied as he unfolded the note. "And our ride." He turned the scrap of paper Levi's direction so he could see the *12* scribbled in orange crayon. He clasped Levi's free hand and tugged him toward the stream of people.

David, however, was planted to the spot, halting their attempt to move. His hard eyes were locked on Marsh. "You said you wouldn't hurt my dad."

"David," Levi gently chided.

Marsh dropped his duffels and knelt in front of David. Midday sun streamed in through the concourse's glass roof, catching every silver strand in Marsh's dark hair like the moonlight had in the bedroom last night, Levi awake long after Marsh had fallen asleep draped across his body. Last night, those rumpled silver strands slipping between his fingers had helped settle Levi, had eased him down from a high he hadn't felt in far too long, had quieted any doubts that what he'd asked for had been too much or that what he and Marsh had done was somehow a betrayal. Nothing so beautiful, nothing so intimate, so good and warm and safe could be a betrayal. But in the light of day—this day—those silver strands reminded Levi of the Stetson that was missing. The one that had been confiscated as evidence, along with the chess set it and Marsh had saved from exploding. Intimacy and safety shattered. His other hat was packed in the duffel on the ground beside Marsh, tucked away where it couldn't draw attention to the escape they were trying to make without detection. But even without his hat, Marsh stared up at David with the same determined cowboy look he'd given Levi three weeks ago from across the table in that restaurant. "I did," Marsh said, "and I failed."

"*You* didn't hurt me," Levi said. "And you didn't fail. I'm right here." He stepped forward, a hand on Marsh's shoulder, his other arm still around David, moving them all closer together. "We're all right here."

Marsh lifted his gaze, meeting his eyes, his dark brown ones full of blame, one hundred percent directed at himself.

"I saw your face when we realized David had the chess set meant for us. I suspect you've only been that afraid one other time in your life. That *hurt*, so yeah, I failed." Levi wanted to drop to the ground and hug him. Run his hand through Marsh's hair again and return some of the comfort —some of the confidence—Marsh had breathed into his life the past few weeks. But Levi didn't, not in the crowded concourse and not when it was his son who needed a boost more right now, which Marsh also understood, speaking directly to David again. "I failed, but I will not fail again."

"Why can't we stay here with Nonna and Pop?"

"It's safer for us to go and for them to stay," Levi said. "Aunt Liz will keep them and the rest of the family safe." He'd never been so happy for his aunt's extravagant wealth as he had been that morning, ushering his entire family behind the heavy metal gates of Liz's massive estate.

"They're like the wing pawns," Marsh said. "We want to keep them away from the middle of the board, away from the action."

"Where we are." The wobble in David's voice betrayed the fear underlying his anger.

"Not for long," Marsh said as he stood. "We're retreating to our safe squares, to a place where neither of you"—he split a glance between them—"will be hurt."

"How can you be sure?"

"I can't be, not one hundred percent, but my moms' ranch is the safest place I know, and they're both pretty fucking scary with their shotguns."

"Moms? As in plural?"

Marsh cracked the first smile Levi had seen from him since early that morning before everything had gone to shit. "Two of them, and they're a hoot. I think they'd like to meet you." Shared some of that smile with Levi too. "Both of you."

"I'll follow your lead," Levi said to David, following Marsh's lead and putting some of the power back in David's hands.

It worked, David straightening his back and shrugging off Levi's arm. "Which gate?"

"Twelve."

David grabbed his rolling suitcase with one hand, clasped Levi's hand with the other, stronger than Levi knew his son was capable of, and started moving forward again, barely giving Levi time to grab his own suitcase. Marsh hung back, covering their six, only drawing even again with Levi as they neared the gate. Close enough to whisper in his ear, "No matter what happens with us and this case, you are an amazing father who raised an amazing kid."

They were so close, and David's attention forward, that Levi chanced a brush of his lips against Marsh's. "Thank you."

As Gate 12 came into view, so did Brax, standing in the open doorway to the jetway. He spoke to the gate attendant, who smiled politely and stepped aside to let their group through. "Colonel," Brax greeted with a nod.

"Colonel," Marsh returned, their correct ranks and far more formal than Levi was used to seeing them interact.

For the benefit of the second gate agent, Levi realized, when they reached the other end of the jetway and boarded the plane. And for the benefit of keeping calm, Levi guessed, the toddler who came barreling Marsh's direction as soon as the plane door was closed. "Tesas!"

Levi and David cleared out of the aisle and Marsh ditched his bag and got his arms down in the nick of time, saving the child from a head to knee collision. "Sweet-heart!" he exclaimed, as he scooped her up. All cheers and smiles for the little one, even if it didn't reach his eyes. "I missed you!"

"Missed you too." She gave Marsh a smacking kiss to the cheek... then smacked the same cheek with her hand. "Ba-Ba says you in trouble."

David snickered from across the aisle. "I like her."

"She takes after her aunt," Brax said as he extended his hand David's direction. "Braxton Kane. I'm an old friend of Marsh's."

"David Bishop."

"Nice to meet you, David. This is my daughter, Lily," he said, tickling the toddler's heel.

She squealed and wriggled out of Marsh's arms. "I gonna tell Daddy Tesas is here." She spun toward the back of the plane, then spun right back around and marched over to David. "You got red hair like me!"

"I do," David said. "Wish mine was darker like yours, though."

"Like Daddy." She grabbed him by the hand. "I show you." And in a win that Levi desperately needed today, David graciously followed after her, a far cry from the teen who'd called his little cousin a wanker three weeks ago.

Amy had been right; it wasn't only Levi who'd needed Marsh.

"I see she still hasn't gotten the hang of X," Marsh said to Brax.

"I'm still Ba-Ba, and you're still Tesas. Deal with it."

Brax drew him into one of their back-slapping hugs, and Levi felt no stirrings of jealousy like before. He knew Marsh better now, knew how closely he held those he considered dear and was happy to be counted among them. He waited for them to part before extending his hand to Brax. "It's good to see you again, and thanks for the lift."

Brax jutted a thumb at Marsh. "He put me on standby after the wedding."

Marsh chuffed. "So little faith."

"I had faith you'd find trouble."

The door at the front of the plane opened and the copilot stuck his head out of the cockpit. "We're next to taxi."

Brax nodded, then once the door was closed again, tilted his head toward the back of the plane. "I'm going to go see what trouble they're getting up to." Levi followed his gaze and spied a mountain of a man on the back bench seat. Holt Madigan. Levi recognized him from Marsh's desktop photo, but that digital picture did not do the man's size justice. Or maybe that was just the passage of years between then and now. Somehow, impossibly, he was bigger than Marsh, and the bright tattoos on his bulging arm not holding Lily were the sole focus of David's attention, Levi's son pointing at designs and Holt nodding, speaking animatedly about them, though Levi couldn't pick out the words from this distance over the engine revving. "I'll make sure he's buckled in." Brax said. "We'll talk when we're in the air."

He squeezed Marsh's shoulder, then headed toward the back of the plane. Marsh veered into the closest row of seats and fell into the one beside the window.

"You doing okay?" Levi asked as he buckled into the seat beside him, increasingly worried about Marsh's silence, the downturned corners of his mouth, the faraway look in his eyes that only deepened as the airplane thundered down the runway.

They'd checked in with each other throughout the morning, after each interrogation, and after every phone call. Marsh had claimed to be okay, had been a rock for him and David, but now, when the world was no longer watching, he'd stabled the cocky cowboy persona. Levi was both overjoyed that Marsh had let him see and overwhelmed at the weariness laid bare. Laid bare himself by the words Marsh uttered as he ran a thumb over the ring on Levi's left hand. "Once we get to Texas, if you want to take this off and ditch this whole stupid plan—"

"No way in hell." Not after Marsh had spent the past six hours moving heaven and earth to make his family safe. Not after he'd saved his son this morning and Levi's heart last night. Not after the past three weeks of tireless exceptional work that had closed Levi's case and significantly advanced Marsh's. "And your plan was not stupid." He curled his fingers around Marsh's and with his other hand, grasped Marsh's chin, forcing his gaze. "It worked. You said our enemies would respond with deterrence, retribution, or solicitation. Two out of three."

"At what cost? I made a massive miscalculation. Bell is dead, Greg and Amanda are missing, Matt and Gail are in the hospital, Kwan is in cuffs, David—" He tried to shake away, and when Levi didn't let him go, closed his eyes instead.

Levi sensed the weight in those heavy lids, eased his grip on Marsh's chin, and cupped his cheek. "I'm an FBI agent. I knew the risks the day I signed up for the job and the day you walked into that restaurant."

"But we're right back where we started." He opened his eyes, dark with the burdens of fear and defeat. "A dead draw."

"No, baby," Levi said. "The money showed their hand, just like you wanted them too." Eder Capital. The company who had funded terrorism and trafficking, who'd cost Marsh a friend and boss and Levi months of his life. Who had brought them together. And in the past three weeks they'd unraveled EC's joint operation with Orchard, disrupted their money laundering scheme, saved five women, and had leads on the whereabouts of more victims and EC's facilitator, Stefan Sanders. "We're so much further than when and where we started. Any other interpretation is a miscalculation."

"We got too close." Marsh shook his head, a tear escaping his eye. Levi's heart stopped, skating the razor's edge of Marsh's words, the implications potentially devastating. "I could've lost you and David."

Levi's heart beat again, and he heaved a sigh of relief. "You didn't. We're right here." He used the same words he had with David, aiming to instill the same confidence, to give back to Marsh a little of the confidence he'd given to him and David since he'd swaggered into their lives. He drew Marsh closer, foreheads touching. "The money showed their hand. And they showed me you." He brushed his lips against his husband's, breathing the swagger he'd borrowed back into its rightful owner. He needed the man who could wrestle a steer or suspect to the ground, who could wear a cowboy hat or wield it to save a life, who could hack a bitcoin scheme and leverage it into two case-busting leads, who could be the husband and partner Levi needed in his life, his home, and his bed. He needed Marsh to get back on the horse and take the next steps forward with him. "Time to cowboy up, Agent Marshall."

Want more Marsh & Levi?
Their story continues in *Bad Bishop*, coming Fall 2022!

And if you missed Marsh's previous appearances, be
sure to catch him in *Silent Knight* and *What We
May Be*.

For all the latest updates on new projects, sneak
peeks, and more, sign up for Layla's Newsletter and
join the Layla's Lushes Reader Group on Facebook.

Reviews are an invaluable tool when it comes to spreading
the word about great reads. Please consider leaving an
honest review for *Dead Draw* on your favorite review site.

Thank you for reading!

ACKNOWLEDGMENTS

And we're off and running with Marsh and Levi! These two are such a joy to write, and I owe it to you, Readers, especially my Lushes, for giving Marsh all the love in *Silent Knight* and *What We May Be* and for propelling him to the front of the WIP line. It was the right choice, on so many levels, and thanks for helping me make it!

Thanks as well to the team who helped make this book possible: Wander Aguiar + Rodiney Santiago + Cate Ashwood for the cover magic, Kristi Yanta for confirming I still knew what I was doing and providing that perfect nugget of editorial wisdom that brought it all together, Susie Selva for the timely and expert edits and for being an amazing cheerleader and friend, Lori Parks for the eagle-eye proofreading, Kim and Rachel for the excellent beta input, Kim for all the PA awesomeness, Christian Leatherman for bringing Marsh to audio life both past and present, Nina and the VPR Team for holding my hand as I moved my self-pub backlist and this new release wide, and to everyone who's had a hand in getting the word out about this and all my books. Thank you, thank you, thank you!

Finally, a huge thank you to the author friends who cheered and encouraged and sprinted and sent ARCs these past six months. Your friendship, support, and creativity have kept me afloat, more than you can possibly know. All my love and gratitude.

ALSO BY LAYLA REYNE

For the most up-to-date list of titles and a helpful reading order, please visit www.laylareyne.com.

Fog City:

Prince of Killers

King Slayer

A New Empire

Queen's Ransom

Silent Knight

Agents Irish and Whiskey:

Single Malt

Cask Strength

Barrel Proof

Tequila Sunrise

Trouble Brewing:

Imperial Stout

Craft Brew

Noble Hops

Standalone Titles:

Variable Onset

What We May Be

Changing Lanes:

Relay

Medley

Table for Two:

The Last Drop

Dine With Me

Free Stories:

Blended Whiskey

Final Gravity

Sweater Weather

Freestyle

ABOUT THE AUTHOR

Layla Reyne is the author of *What We May Be* and the *Perfect Play*, *Fog City*, *Agents Irish and Whiskey*, and *Trouble Brewing* series. A Carolina Tar Heel who now calls California home, Layla enjoys weaving her bicoastal experiences into her stories, along with adrenaline-fueled suspense and heart pounding romance.

You can find Layla at laylareyne.com, in her reader group on Facebook—Layla's Lushes, and at the following sites:

facebook.com/laylareyne

twitter.com/laylareyne

instagram.com/laylareyne

bookbub.com/authors/layla-reyne